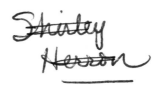

Amish Trust

(Amish Bed & Breakfast, Book 1)

Ruth Hartzler

LARGE PRINT

Chapter 1

It was a rainy, spring morning in Ohio. Rachel considered that there was hope for at least some sunshine to take the chill from the air as the sun crept its way over the hills, only to be hidden again moments later by thick, gray clouds.

Rachel and her mother, Miriam, huddled together on an old wooden bench at the bus terminal in an attempt to keep warm. There were only a few other people waiting to catch the same bus; they all stood, arms crossed, shivering. There were two other wooden benches available, but those were more exposed to the uncharacteristic chill breeze that cut through the air.

Rachel looked around once again. The terminal was an old, brick building and not well kept. There was graffiti on the wall, along with quite a few cracks running up the walls, and inside, the ceiling had strange stains as well as an unpleasant odor. The air was stale with the smell of tuna and egg salad sandwiches. Rachel assumed that the smell came from one of two vending machines in the corner of the room. A small television sat in the top right hand corner of the room and was covered by large sheet paper that read:

Out of Order - The Manager.

Despite being cold, Rachel was excitedly looking forward to seeing to see the house that would be their new home in Pennsylvania, despite the unfortunate event that had left her mother, Miriam, with "Eden," a large home on acres of farmland. Miriam's mother-in-law, Clara, had recently passed away and left Eden to her. Rachel had never met her *grossmammi*, at least, not as far as she could remember.

Rachel snapped back to reality as an old speaker just above their heads crackled to life. A dreary voice spoke, only to choke on something before coughing loudly. The owner of the voice cleared her throat and started again. "Bus direct to Pennsylvania will be arriving in five minutes." She coughed again into the microphone, before turning it off.

"Do you have everything?" Miriam asked, handing a bus ticket to Rachel.

Rachel took the ticket from Miriam's shaking hand and laughed. "Let's hope the bus driver has the heat on," she said.

As the bus appeared on the horizon, they stood and straightened themselves up to join the makeshift line forming to board the bus. After they were seated, Rachel turned to Miriam. "How long will it take?"

Miriam looked at her ticket. "Let me see. Oh, about six and a half hours."

Rachel rested her elbow on the edge of the bus window to support her head and sighed. "They could have given us more leg room," she said, while shifting her legs to get comfortable. "Though it's better than being out there."

They both looked out the window, and Rachel wiped her hand along it to remove the fog. The day looked sad, gray and miserable. The fog slowly stretched itself along the window, blocking her view, and as it did so, she turned away and slumped back into her seat.

By the time the bus was out of the city and cruising along the long stretch of highway, Rachel had drifted off to sleep. She must have slept for hours, as she awoke to the green, rolling hills of Pennsylvania. "Are we almost there?" she asked her *mudder*, followed by, "Are you all right?"

Miriam was sitting upright in her seat, her brow creased. "I'm just anxious about starting a B&B," she said.

Rachel nodded. "I'm nervous, too. It's not just leaving Ohio and moving to Pennsylvania," she said, "but it's starting a whole new life. I've left all my friends behind. I've never known anything different, and now, we're starting afresh."

Miriam's face relaxed. "We'll soon get used to the community there. It's not unlike ours, going by the letters I've exchanged with the bishop. They are so kind. He told me that the community will make sure the refrigerator is running, and stock it with essentials for us. He even wrote that they'll have two bedrooms prepared for us." She sighed. "It's been such a struggle for me for years, running the farm ever since you were a *boppli* when your *vadder* left this life and went to be with *Der Herr*."

Rachel nodded. She was too young to remember her father, or his passing in a farm accident.

"A B&B will be hard work, of course," her *mudder* continued, "but not as hard as dealing with contracts and lease farmers, and all the hard physical work around the farm." She rubbed her shoulder as she spoke. "Your *grossmammi's* house is just the right size to turn into a B&B, and it has lovely views over a creek and fields. I hope to be able to lease out the farmland, long term, to the one farmer, and hopefully, an Amish farmer, not to various *Englischers* on a short term basis like I'm used to doing. Everything will be just fine. You wait and see."

Rachel smiled in reassurance, but, truth be told, she was more than a little worried about her mother's plans to open a B&B in a strange community, in a new place. Rachel shook herself and forced her fears aside. *How bad could it be?* she asked herself, as the bus drew ever closer to their destination.

Just over an hour later, Rachel and her *mudder* were standing on the side of the road looking at their new home. Their jaws had dropped, and their eyes bulged wide. All the blood had drained from their faces. They stared in utter shock and disbelief at the sight.

Chapter 2

The whole scene before them was one of decay and neglect. The wood on the outside had changed from what looked like the original deep brown to a peeling gray; the roof bore holes, while the windows were cracked and dusty. What was supposed to be the flower bed sprouted naked thorns with sharp prickles, surrounded by parched, overgrown grass. The trees surrounding the large house were bare, weak, and begging for hydration.

"I can't believe this place looks like this!" Rachel said. "*Mamm*, what will we do?"

"Hopefully inside won't be as bad," Miriam said with a catch in her voice. "Besides, it's in a great location. Visitors come in and out of the area often, especially during the holidays when people want a break from the city. I'm sure they're often forced to stay in musty, overpriced hotels and travel five miles to the nearest McDonalds for breakfast. I have no doubt that the venture will be a success.

Rachel, the location's ideal! Just look at the beautiful view." She waved her hand expansively.

Rachel followed the direction in which her mother was pointing, but it was hard to for her to pay attention to the beautiful creek and rolling fields. Instead, all she could focus on was the large, decrepit house.

Miriam was still speaking. "Guests will think of this as the perfect weekend getaway! I can't wait to get it up and running. I'll just have to get someone to cut the lawn and repair the peeling wood and roof. Rachel, in no time the *haus* will be looking brand new!"

Miriam's enthusiasm was beginning to rub off on Rachel, that is, until Miriam turned the door handle, and the pair stepped inside their new home.

The inside of the house looked like a tornado passed through it, not once, but perhaps a couple of times. The interior was completely turned upside down. Rachel at first was too stunned to move from her position by the door. The entrance and the living room looked as if they had been thoroughly completely.

Boards and cupboards dangled from the rusting counters, while the sink was coated black. The floor in parts appeared to be eaten by rodents, and the peeling window panes encased cracked glass. Holes from the ceiling formed little puddles on the eroding floors. A detestable stench emanated from the kitchen, signaling the presence of rotten food and spoiled liquid. Rachel at once put her hand over her nose.

Rachel followed Miriam into the living room. It contained a worn out, mutilated sofa, a sofa in better condition, a small rectangular table, a few chairs, and a cracked television set. The old carpet sent a gruesome, filthy scent into the air. Stacks of dusty old books perched on shelves by the walls and the fan above dangled precariously from the ceiling.

Rachel let out a deep sigh. "*Mamm*, what are we going to do?"

Miriam, however, did not reply. She was too busy muttering to herself. "This place is a disaster, what – how - I don't understand? Why wasn't I told?"

Rachel was unable to offer any words of encouragement. She had anticipated a few repairs around the house before transforming the space into a B&B, but never had she imagined that she would be undertaking a home construction job. The magnitude of the work to be done made her head spin, and she started to feel dizzy.

Rachel let out a deep sigh. "Can we even stay here for the night? I'm worried about what we'll find upstairs," she said. "Where are we going to sleep?"

Miriam shook her head. "The bishop's had two rooms prepared for us. Let's have a look around the rest of the place first. We need to make a list of all the necessary supplies for each room - everything from tiles, curtains, paint, and wallpaper. Then we need to make a list of all the bedding, and any furniture that needs replacing. I want the Bed and Breakfast to have a bright and cozy feeling."

Rachel held back her comments. She was overwhelmed at the state of the home, and could not see how her *mudder* was being so optimistic.

Miriam hurried up the staircase, while Rachel walked around the ragged kitchen and worn out living room, jotting down notes on the necessary tools to transform each space. Although there was plenty of natural light, it did not help the dilapidated look of the place.

"Okay, I think I have everything covered upstairs," Miriam said, as soon as she returned. "It's not as bad as I thought. The bathrooms are actually in a good state of repair, and everything upstairs just needs a good clean. Our bedrooms have been prepared. At least we'll have somewhere to sleep tonight."

Rachel shuddered at the thought of sleeping in the house. "Will we take a look outside?"

Miriam nodded her agreement.

The scene outside their home was truly a beautiful sight. The rolling hills kissed the horizon as the sun beamed above the lush grass. There was not a cloud in the sky. The air was peaceful and the atmosphere was tranquil.

"I think we can create a lovely garden here, Rachel. We can plant some roses, add a few chairs and benches. I also want to add a few tables with garden umbrellas. What are your plans for the living room?"

Rachel tapped her forehead. "I was thinking that the sofas need to be replaced, but some of the furniture just needs a good clean.

The ceiling fan needs to be replaced. We could add French doors that open up to the patio."

Miriam's face fell. "It all takes money, and Clara didn't leave us much, only enough to have the electricity connected and the phone."

"Oh yes. The bishop gave his permission then?" Rachel knew that Amish businesses, unlike their private homes, were generally permitted to have electricity, phone, and even internet connected, but Miriam had not told her that the bishop of this community had already given his permission. Of course, her mother wouldn't have had the idea of a B&B if he hadn't.

Miriam nodded, and continued talking. "I have no idea where Clara was living – clearly not here. Anyway, let's check out the horse and buggy."

Rachel clutched at her stomach. She had not thought about the horse and buggy – if Clara had not left them a horse and buggy, they would have no means of transport. She looked up to see Miriam staring at her.

"Don't worry, Rachel. I know the house is a big disappointment, but the will clearly stated that the horse is sound and the buggy is in good repair."

I'll believe it when I see it, Rachel thought, but she simply nodded. When the two walked out to the pasture behind the house, there indeed was fine looking, bay mare with a perfect, white star on her face. As soon as the mare saw them, she trotted up.

"I expect she wants a carrot," Rachel said, stroking the mare's face. "I wonder who's been looking after her?"

"The bishop said he would have someone look after her. Let's look at the barn."

The barn was in far better condition than the house. There was even a phone inside, but it was not working. *Like everything else in this place*, Rachel thought with dismay.

Chapter 3

The following morning, the two were driving the bay mare into town. As they drove down the road amidst the early morning sun, Rachel inhaled the crisp, pure air. She looked at the lush grass and the long stretch of open road kissing the horizon. Perhaps the place wasn't so bad, after all. The upstairs did have two habitable bedrooms.

The hardware store was bigger than Rachel had expected, and it took Rachel and Miriam over an hour to select the essentials within their tight budget.

"I think we have everything," Miriam said, her tone indicating that she was overwhelmed.

The two stood in line at the checkout and waited patiently. There was a tall, Amish man in front of them, and Rachel assumed that the three would exchange introductions once he turned around.

When the *mann* did turn around, Rachel sucked in a sharp breath. He had piercing green eyes, tanned, chiseled features, and wavy, brown hair stuck out from under his hat. Rachel's heart raced.

"You should never have been allowed in town! You don't belong here!" he snapped, his green eyes piercing. Then in one swift motion, he grabbed his purchases, and bolted out the door.

Rachel's and Miriam's mouths dropped open in shock at his outburst.

"Who is he?" Miriam asked the store assistant.

"You don't know him?" she asked. "I mean, being Amish and all." Her voice trailed away.

"We only arrived in town yesterday," Miriam said. "We're just moved here from Ohio."

The store assistant nodded. "That's Isaac Petersheim. Ever since his wife left some time back, he's completely changed. I wouldn't take it personally." She rang up their receipt and handed it to them.

Rachel was confused by Isaac's words. "Why did he speak to us like that?" she asked Miriam.

Miriam shrugged. "And what did the store assistant mean saying by his wife left? She said *left*, not *died*."

It was Rachel's turn to shrug. "Perhaps that's how *Englischers* in these parts talk about someone dying," she said.

"Perhaps." Miriam did not seem quite so sure. "Rachel, if you wouldn't mind, I'll take all this to the buggy, if you would get the groceries. The grocery store is just there." She pointed to a grocery store nearby, and then handed Rachel a list.

Rachel was searching the shelves when she saw the same tall, Amish man, Isaac Petersheim. He was heading her way, and Rachel hoped that his boiling temper had subsided and that he would be able to communicate in a more civil manner.

Isaac looked shocked to see Rachel. His eyes were stern.

"What do you want?" he said as she approached him.

Rachel was shocked by his reaction. Clearly his temper had not subsided as she had anticipated. He was still as outraged and wrathful.

"Why are you so angry with my *familye*?" she said.

"Are you serious? You really don't know?" He stared at her with open hostility.

At the same time, Rachel refused to let Isaac intimidate her. She was not afraid of him or his harsh words. She folded her arms and stared at him.

"Didn't your *mudder* tell you anything about how she treated your *grossmammi*, Clara?" he continued. "She left her mother-in-law in that old, dilapidated house."

Rachel's jaw dropped with the revelation. She was in utter shock.

"Yes, your *mudder* left your *grossmammi* here all alone in that old house," he pressed on. "It was left to the community to care for Clara. I got her medication, bought her groceries, and even cooked for her until she moved in with the Schwartz *familye*, while your *mudder* did not even visit, not even once. Your *familye* is a disgrace to the community and should never have been allowed back here."

Rachel could not help the wave of sadness, disappointment and shock that rippled through her. She could not believe what she was hearing. Why would her mother treat Clara that way? There had to be a logical explanation. "Listen Isaac, I'm sure there's a perfectly good explanation for my *mudder's* actions. My *mudder* is a kind and loving person. She -"

Isaac abruptly cut her off. "No, *you* listen! Your *mudder* is a mean and selfish woman. As a matter of fact, your whole *familye* is." Isaac's dark green eyes bore into her soul and she diverted her eyes from him for a brief moment. Isaac Petersheim was a furious *mann*, that was for sure, and for the second time that day, and she was at the brunt of another of his angry tirades. Yet when she looked deeper, she saw pain in his eyes and hurt in his soul. There was a lot more to his anger than his feelings as to how Miriam had treated Clara, of that she was sure.

Isaac was still talking, his tone angry. "Clara was nothing like your *mudder* or the rest of your *familye*. Your *familye* treated her like trash but she was still nice enough to leave you her *haus*. You people don't appreciate anything, and it's sad that such a nice lady like Clara had such a mean spirited family."

"That's enough, Mr. Petersheim!" Rachel snapped. "I will not have you talk about my *familye* in that way!"

Isaac turned around and made to leave, but then turned to face Rachel again. "Your *familye* doesn't care about anyone. It's time for you to open your eyes and see it for yourself."

Before Rachel even had the chance to respond, he was gone in the same angry fashion in which he had exited the hardware store. Rachel paid for her groceries and then hurried to the buggy. Miriam was already waiting in the buggy.

Rachel couldn't wait to tell Miriam what had happened." I just spoke to Isaac Petersheim again. He told me that you didn't take care of *Grossmammi* Clara before she died."

Miriam let out a long sigh, and tears welled up in her eyes. "Oh, Rachel, I knew I'd have to tell you all this one day. Your *grossmammi* was very strict with your *vadder* when he was growing up. In fact, she was so strict that it drove your father away from home. He was the only child she had, and her own husband died when your *vadder* was quite young. As soon as your *vadder* turned eighteen, he moved to our community in Ohio. In fact, it was at his bishop's suggestion."

Rachel listened in disbelief. She had no idea that her *vadder* had endured such a difficult upbringing. "Is that why I have never met my *grossmammi*? It must have been awful to be sick and living in this house all alone," she said softly.

"I'm sorry you never met your *grossmammi*, Rachel," Miriam said. "Your *vadder* was estranged from her, and once he went to be with *Gott*, I felt it would've been against his wishes to take you to see her. I had never met her. She didn't come to our wedding."

"Did she know about me?" Rachel asked.

"*Jah*." Miriam nodded. "After you were born, your father and I sent her a letter letting her know, and asking if she would to come and see her grandchild. Yet she did not respond to that letter or to any other letters that we sent. Your *vadder* finally gave up sending letters. He said it was probably for the best, that we should keep you as far away from her as possible, because he didn't want her to impose her strict rules on us and tell us what a bad parents we were. But looking back, I should've tried harder. I should have at least given you the chance to know her. I am so sorry."

Chapter 4

Isaac Petersheim stormed out of the hardware store amidst a sea of shocked expressions. He did not apologize for his outburst and he did not look back. Instead, he hopped into his buggy and clicked his horse into a fast trot down the road. He gripped the reins with tense fingers, his eyebrows knitted together and his face stern and red. The rage had started when the news that they were coming had been announced in the community, and had been boiling inside him ever since he had spotted Miriam and Rachel in the store. He tried to control his temper while he shopped, but when he had reached the cashier and was only a few inches away from the pair, he had erupted.

He simply could not leave without giving them a piece of his mind. "Do they think people forgot how badly they treated Clara?" he said aloud, as he pushed his horse on faster. "Miriam Burkholder has no right to be in town. She should turn around and head straight back to where she came from!"

Isaac liked the quiet solitude of his lonely existence. He liked living alone, and only venturing out when he had to go to town, or to the church meetings every second Sunday. Even then, he did not stay for the meal, but hurried home.

Yet something else had happened back there in the store that he wasn't prepared for and he was not even sure how to explain it to himself. In the fleeting moment when he whipped around to unleash his fury on Miriam, he noticed Rachel's brown eyes, and lovely brown hair poking out from under her bonnet. The sight of her set him slightly off guard, and for a moment he regretted his actions toward them. Nevertheless, he bore such a deep resentment for Miriam and the way she had treated Clara during her illness, that he refused to entertain any feelings for her daughter.

When his wife left him three years earlier, he buried love, feelings, intimacy, and romance in a deep, dark hole. He had no intentions of ever unearthing those sentiments again. He had resigned himself to a life of solitude, that was exactly the way it was going to stay.

Isaac made his way down the long, winding road to his large farm a few miles outside town. His irritation subsided, and his temper cooled. His shoulders were now more relaxed, and he was a lot less tense. Now, as he approached a more comfortable and familiar scene, he was more composed. He left home that morning to purchase a few supplies for the new chicken coop he was building at the back of the house. He had not expected to get into a confrontation and he had not expected to be attracted to a stranger. The morning had taken an unexpected turn, and he was glad to be home.

After seeing to his horse, Isaac opened his front gate and was immediately greeted by a happy border collie.

"Hey, Spot," Isaac said, ruffling the dog's hair, as Spot jumped up on his hind legs. "I missed you too," Isaac said with a smile.

The sun's bright rays illuminated the sky and hovered over the lush setting. It was a majestic scene, one that made him nostalgic. Today, he had been unable to control his emotions, and deep down, that frustrated him. It made him realize he was still angry with the world, and there was more to his outburst than how Miriam had treated Clara.

Just three years ago, this farm was alive and flourishing. He and his ex-wife, Olivia, had lived a humble but blissful life. Olivia had been a hard worker, picking the vegetables she had planted, and feeding their pigs, cows and chickens. To Isaac, she had been the most beautiful, loving, and kind woman in the world. They had both enjoyed their simple and peaceful country life. That was, until the life they had shared was no longer good enough for her.

Isaac remembered the moment everything changed. It had started as a lovely, Sunday morning. Olivia had complained about a headache, but insisted that Isaac go to the church meeting without her.

Yet instead of arriving home to see his wife there, he had come back to an empty house. Isaac made his way around the back of their home to the barn, but all he saw were cows, horses, and chickens staring back at him.

He made his way back into the house calling his wife's name, but got no response. Just then, he noticed a parked car down the road. The car was barely visible, as it was almost completely hidden by the tall trees surrounding the farm. The color and model looked familiar. It closely resembled the car driven by Mark Lambert, the owner of the furniture store where Olivia worked part time as a seamstress, but what on earth would Mark be doing hiding behind the bushes across from his house?

Isaac remembered how his heart had raced and how a nervous sweat had formed on his forehead. His knees had grown weak and he paced the floor and then the realization hit him. At that moment, Olivia stepped through the door, her hair muffled, and her face flushed.

"Where have you been?" he asked sternly.

"Oh, I was just out for a walk," she said casually.

"Is that is Mark Lambert's car parked down the side road?"

Olivia let out a deep sigh. "He just came by to talk about the schedule for next week."

"On a Sunday?" Isaac snapped.

"Yes, on a Sunday." By this time, Olivia was done with the conversation; she was already making her way upstairs, slamming the bedroom door behind her.

This was a side of his *fraa* that Isaac had never experienced. The next morning, when Isaac went into the house for lunch, he intended to have a good talk with Olivia. He found a note on the dining room table. It was blunt, to the point, and heartbreaking all at the same time.

I don't love you anymore. I have left with Mark.

I want a divorce, Olivia.

Isaac ran into the bedroom. All Olivia's items were missing from the bathroom along with her clothes from the closet. The house was completely void of all his wife's belongings.

And just like that, she was gone. Over the next three years, he never heard a single word from her. She never returned to town or to the home they shared. She was, of course, shunned from the community. The only thing he heard was from her lawyer, hastening him to sign the divorce papers to she could marry Mark Lambert. Rumor had it that Mark Lambert and Olivia had moved into a beachside condo in California. Isaac had no idea that Olivia had been dissatisfied with their marriage, let alone with the Amish life.

Five years of marriage had come tumbling down in just a few days. When Olivia left, she took their dreams and a piece of his soul with him. Isaac spent the next three years alone, depressed, bitter and detached from his community. He lost all desire to tend to the farm they had built together. In fact he lost all zest for life.

Isaac let out a deep sigh when the sun became obscured by clouds, and the sky turned dark. His trip into the past had cast an even grayer cloud over an already tumultuous day.

Isaac's home was a direct reflection of his life. His home was dark and gloomy and lacked the warmth and love it had radiated during his marriage to Olivia. As far as Isaac was concerned, all life had completely been sucked out of the *haus*. Now it had turned into his cave to shut out the world.

Chapter 5

A loud thud reverberated through the large home.

"*Mamm*, someone's at the door." Rachel jumped to her feet and walked toward the front of the house, with Miriam hard on her heels. When she pulled the door open, she saw an older couple standing on her steps. They wore big smiles, and the lady was holding a big plate of pies.

The man had a long, white beard and a no-nonsense manner, but his warm eyes made Rachel feel at ease. "My name is Herman Byler. I'm the bishop around these parts." Smiling, he turned and nodded to his wife. "This is my *fraa*, Lydia. We wanted to welcome you both to the community."

Miriam invited them to come inside. As they stepped into the entrance, Lydia handed Miriam the pie. "Here you are! I baked some whoopie pies." She smiled.

Miriam set the pie on the table and smiled at their guest. "Thank you kindly, Lydia," she said. She led them into the large, dilapidated living room. Miriam indicated that the bishop and his *fraa* should sit on the sofa to the right. It was the less patchy of the two sofas in the room, and Miriam and Rachel sat opposite, on the more damaged sofa. Springs emerged from several of areas of ripped cloth. "This place has seen better days, that's for sure," Miriam said, as they took their seats.

"Would you like some hot garden tea, or perhaps a cold drink?" Miriam asked the guests.

They both opted for a cold drink, so Miriam and Rachel hurried to the kitchen. Rachel poured iced spiced tea into four glasses and then set them upon a tray, while her *mudder* got some plates out of the one good cupboard.

When they returned, Rachel saw that the bishop was looking around, and a solemn look was weighing down his otherwise happy demeanor. "I'm sorry the place is in such bad shape," he said, "but it's been unattended to for quite a while." The bishop looked around the room again. "Have you ladies been settling in well? You will enjoy the community here." He smiled warmly.

"It's been great, *denki*, Bishop Byler," Miriam said. "It will take a little getting used to, but I think we'll love it here."

"Yes, moving from Ohio to Pennsylvania would be difficult for anyone at first," Lydia said.

"Thank you for cleaning out the refrigerator and getting it running, along with preparing the two bedrooms for our arrival. It saved us a lot of hard work. It was nice not to have to attend to that after our long journey," Miriam said.

The bishop's smile faded as he turned to his *fraa*, and then back toward Rachel and her mother. "You're welcome, dear. It was a bit of a task, but what would life be without hard work? Not much fun, eh?"

Rachel found a hint of humor in the bishop's words, and there was something about the kindness in his voice. She glanced at her mother and saw her smiling, clearly feeling a similar emotion.

"That's very true," Miriam said in agreement. "Oh, and we also thank you both for feeding and caring for the horse that my mother-in-law left us. You have already lifted quite some of the burden from our shoulders. Thank you kindly."

"That is what we're here for," Lydia said. She looked over at her husband and they smiled.

"Exactly," the bishop added. "We want to make your stay in the community happy. We hope to become a part of your *familye*, and you both will become a part of ours as well." His smile widened, and his eyes sparkled. "I hope you can make a financial success of Eden."

"*Denki*," Miriam said. "I just hope we can get the place in better shape soon. It's so dilapidated and falling apart. It seems as if nothing has been done to this *haus* in a long time."

"Oh, this damage isn't all from age and lack of repair," the bishop said. "Much of the damage is from the looters."

Rachel and Miriam exchanged glances, clearly confused. "Looters?" they both asked in unison.

"Yes, looters," he said. "They're treasure hunters looking for the treasure of Eden. When this house is left uninhabited, like when your late grandmother moved in with the

Schwartz *familye* when she became ill, the looters come out in droves, searching high and low for signs that it still exists in this location. They think it's still buried here."

Rachel was confused.

"What's the treasure of Eden?" Miriam asked.

"Have you ever heard of Captain Kidd?" the bishop asked.

Rachel had never heard of him, and as her *mudder* was shaking her head, it was apparent that like she had not heard of the man either.

"He commanded a crew of pirates back in the seventeenth

century," the bishop said. "I believe it was the late 1600s when he and his bandits roamed the wild seas, hunting and pillaging any ships they came across. They were known for attacking trade routes head on. Many people believe that several of their pirated treasures may still be buried out in the world, some even being here."

"Herman, perhaps you don't have to go into such detail," Lydia said.

"Yes, I'm sorry," he said, returning a smile.

"No, it's okay," said Miriam. "This is interesting. I do remember that my husband mentioned this to me many years ago, but I don't remember the particulars."

The bishop cleared his throat as he prepared to finish the story. "Anyway, one of Captain Kidd's high ranking officials was supposedly a man named Dr. John Eden. When Captain Kidd was sent to the gallows for his various crimes, Dr. Eden retired to Pennsylvania and built a house in a rural part of town. It became known as Eden's Hill. That is where it is believed that he stored his treasure until he died years later. If it's true and the treasure is mostly untouched, it would be worth a fortune."

"What does that have to do with this house?" Rachel asked, battling her confusion.

"When Dr. Eden died, treasure hunters started pouring over the area, looking for his lost gold," the bishop said. "At first, there were a few visitors per month or so, but as time went on, it's said that they started coming more and more often. Eventually, a young family built a large house on this land. Rumors say that these people had stumbled upon some, if not all, of Dr. Eden's lost gold."

"They named that house *Eden*, and it is the very house in which we are sitting right now," said Lydia.

"Why would they be searching inside the house?" Rachel asked. "If the pirate buried it, wouldn't it be in his original home or deep in the ground?"

The bishop shook his head. "This house was built directly on the location of Dr. Eden's original house. His house was eventually destroyed by looters and left a wasteland, until the young *familye* built this home. At any rate, when you come to the church meeting, we will organize help for you. This is too much work for two people." Bishop Herman had a stern look on his face, but his features were kind and warm.

Miriam smiled. "We appreciate it. *Denki*, Bishop Byler."

"And I'm sure your neighbor, Isaac Petersheim, will be of help. Er is en faehicher schreiner." *He is an able carpenter.*

Rachel and Miriam exchanged glances, a fact which did not escape the bishop's notice.

"Have you met Isaac already?" he asked.

"*Jah*, we have," Miriam said. "He was quite angry with us."

The bishop nodded. "Pay him no mind. He has had a very difficult time. I'm sure he will come around sooner on later, all in *Gott's* timing. *For there is a time and a way for everything, although man's trouble lies heavy on him.* That is from Ecclesiastes, chapter eight, and verse six."

"We should probably be going," Lydia said, standing up abruptly and smiling. "Thank you both for allowing us into your home. I can't wait to see what this place will look like when it's restored and open for business."

The bishop followed her lead and rose to his feet. "Yes, thank you both. It's very rare that we see new faces. It's uncommon for us to welcome new members to our community. Again, if you need anything at all, please don't worry about asking. We're all *familye* around here." The bishop turned and followed his *fraa* to the front door as Rachel and Miriam trailed behind to say their final goodbyes.

As he reached the bishop door, he paused and turned back to Miriam and Rachel. "Please do not be concerned about any looters. They're not criminals, just adventurers looking to find some historical artifacts or gold or whatever is said to be in Eden's treasure. *Grossmammi* Clara lived here for a long time and never had any real problems with them. Once they realize that the *haus* is no longer vacant, they will stop coming." He rubbed his *baard*. "Perhaps, with your permission, I will have some signs made and have them posted around the land just in case."

Miriam thanked him once again, and he hurried to catch up with his *fraa*.

Miriam closed the door and looked at her daughter. "Oh no, we have more things to worry about now."

"I suppose that explains all the holes in the walls," Rachel said.

Miriam wiped away a tear. "We'll have this place restored and ready to open in no time. We can't let a local legend and some treasure hunters ruin what can be a good thing." Miriam smiled, but Rachel could see that she was concerned.

"Don't worry, *Mamm*. The bishop said that the treasure hunters aren't criminals. Once they know that the place is no longer vacant, they'll leave us alone."

Chapter 6

"This house is just a mess," Rachel mumbled to herself as she swept the floor for the umpteenth time. No matter how many times she swept it, it still seemed as if there was just as much dirt to clean up as when she had started.

The sweeping had given Rachel plenty of time to think. The house was supposed to be a fresh start for both Rachel and her *mudder*. They had simply expected to do some minor renovating, and then open the *haus* as a B&B. Yet the house was in appalling condition, and Rachel felt that they had made a mistake in moving there.

Now all their time was consumed with doing all the repairs that they could handle. Once done with those, they would have to hire someone to do the rest. Hopefully an affordable price could be reached for expert help. Until then, it was just the two of them, and the work was tedious as well as hard. Rachel's mother's dream of starting a B&B was now a crazy home improvement affair for which neither woman was prepared. Miriam had band-aids on all her fingers from splinters, and Rachel actually worried that cutting herself on a nail in this place would give her tetanus.

"Why would *Grossmammi* leave the house in shambles?" Rachel asked, as Miriam came into the room with mop and bucket.

"I don't know," Miriam responded, "but we have a place free and clear. No reason to look a gift horse in the mouth just because it needs a little elbow grease. We're not afraid of hard work. Alle Daag rumhersitze macht em faul." *Sitting all day makes one lazy*.

Rachel yawned widely.

"Why don't you get some air?" Miriam said. "Perhaps you could go for a walk through the fields."

"I can't leave you to do the work, *Mamm*."

Miriam waved her hands at Rachel. "Nonsense - off you go! You've been working so hard; you need a break. I'll have to town anyway, so we might as well both stop working for a while."

Rachel walked outside, and then down the little track beside the creek. It was peaceful, but lonely at the same time. Still, she marveled at the beauty of *Gott's* creation, the dozens of wildflowers, the red and yellow bell-shaped flowers of the columbine contrasting with the purple asters.

Rachel wondered if her *mudder* had the best place to start a business, but at least they did own the building free and clear. Rachel sighed. The house did need extensive renovations simply to quality as a *haus*, let alone a proper B&B. Rachel missed her friends back in Ohio, and as yet, had met no one in the community here – apart from the bishop and his *fraa*.

She was a little nervous about the coming church meeting.

Rachel wandered, lost in thought, when she saw an Amish *mann* working on a fence in the distance. As she approached, she saw it was Isaac. *I should've turned back*, she silently scolded herself. *I'd forgotten he was our closest neighbor*. Rachel hesitated for a moment, wondering whether to hurry home or to continue her walk. Suddenly, righteous indignation overcame her and she stomped forward. *Why should I let him intimate me?* she asked herself. *I fear no man, only Gott!*

By the time she reached Isaac, Rachel was ready to give him a piece of her mind. Isaac turned around, and his face paled as he faced Rachel's approach. She did not give him the opportunity to speak. "Listen, you have the wrong idea about my *familye*, and it's time for you to get over all that hatred you have for us. We are *gut* people," Rachel said in a commanding and stern voice.

"I don't hate your *familye*, Rachel," Isaac said softly. "I just don't like the way your *mudder* treated Clara."

Rachel folded her arms across her chest. "You have no idea what it was like for my father growing up. *Grossmammi* Clara was very harsh toward him."

"I know you're right, Rachel, and I'm sorry. Clara often said that she regretted the strict way she had behaved to your *vadder*. I must apologize for the way I lashed out at you." His tone was soft.

Rachel had been expecting an argument, and was shocked by the apology. Isaac had been so mean to her that she had no idea he was capable of displaying any form of sensitivity. She could not help but blush at the way he said her name and the softness in his voice.

Rachel took a faltering step to him, trying to figure out how to respond to his words, when she stumbled in a hole and fell hard. The pain in her right ankle was intense, and it felt as if it were being impaled with sharp rods.

"Are you all right?" Isaac dropped what he was doing and ran over.

"I wasn't watching what I was doing," Rachel said, and then took offense when the corners of his mouth twitched. "I meant I was busy watching you." When Rachel realized how that sounded, she added, "I mean that I was hurrying to you to tell you off for what you said." Rachel felt her cheeks flush hot and she was sure they were beet red.

"Well, right now we need to get you sorted," Isaac said. He offered Rachel his hand. "Let me help you."

As he pulled Rachel to her feet, she let out a little cry of pain. "I twisted it."

"My *haus* is nearby," Isaac said. "If you will let me help you get there, I can put some ice on it and

I'll see if you'll need to go to the *doktor*."

Rachel was mortified. "Fine, but we're walking. You're not carrying me."

Isaac chuckled. "I wouldn't dream of it. Lean on my arm."

By the time they reached Isaac's *haus*, Rachel was on the verge of tears. Isaac wasted no time in taking off her boot. The ankle was swollen. "*Nee*, it's not broken," he said, and then hurried out of the room, returning soon after with an icepack and some aspirin. A grateful Rachel accepted both. The pain started to subside as soon as the icepack was on the ankle.

"So, what exactly were you going to tell me off about?" Isaac asked.

"Well, you did apologize," Rachel said, "but you accused me of abandoning my *grossmammi*. I didn't even know about Clara until after she died. My *mudder* never told me."

"Oh," Isaac said. "I didn't know about that." Isaac crossed to the window to look out. "Now if you can think you can walk a little, I'll get the buggy and drive you home."

* * *

Isaac was uncomfortable with a woman in his *haus*, and an attractive woman at that. The only woman who had been in his house since Olivia was the bishop's wife.

After Olivia left him, Isaac figured it was in *Gott's* plan for him to live alone for the rest of his life. He was not attracted to any of the Amish women in the community. Who would have thought an Amish woman would arrive from another community, and at that, an Amish woman with whom he had undeniable chemistry?

Isaac thought of the Scripture in the book of Isaiah, *For my thoughts are not your thoughts, neither are your ways my ways, declares the Lord.*

What did *Gott* have in store for him? Isaac thought he'd had his whole life planned, but perhaps *Gott* had other ideas.

Chapter 7

"Are you all right?" Miriam asked, as she and Rachel carefully made their way across the fields.

"I'm all right." Rachel gave her *mudder* a smile of reassurance as she balanced the cake pan in her hands. She was fine, or at least she would be fine until she got there. Then it would remain to be seen. Rachel did not know what to make of her neighbor. First he was completely hostile, and then almost sweet, and then he was again cold and distant. She had no idea if they would be meeting the nice *mann* or the angry hermit when they got there.

Granted, Rachel had said harsh words the previous day, but what was she supposed to do? Pretend that treating her like he had was okay? Come to think of it, what was wrong with her? Amish did not confront people. They did not complain when they were wronged. If the cashier had a bad attitude, Rachel would simply thank them for her change and then go on about her life. If someone made it personal, she tried to avoid them.

She did not go running down to a field to give them a piece of her mind. What was it about Isaac Petersheim that got under her skin like this?

"Are you sure you're up to this?" her *mudder* asked again. "If your ankle is still hurting, I'm sure Mr. Petersheim will understand if you stayed home."

"I'll be fine," Rachel said in response, hoping her voice did not sound too desperate. When she had told her *mudder* about how Isaac had helped her, she seemed so happy. Miriam had been thrilled that the *mann* was warming up to them and had helped her *dochder*.

Rachel listened to her *mudder's* plans for the week the rest of the way to Isaac's *haus*. Despite everything that had happened yesterday, Rachel still had managed to take in the appearance of the place. It was remarkably well kept, especially for a lonely bachelor. There was not a weed to be seen, and the wooden porch looked as if it had been given a fresh coat of wood stain recently. The back field had some cattle plodding lazily along in a huge pasture, and Rachel had heard the faint sound of chickens somewhere nearby. Even the barn looked neat and clean, at least from the outside.

In fact, Isaac's *haus* was neat and trim, and surprisingly inviting for a place owned by an angry hermit. And this man had delivered her home, to a *haus* complete with weeds and loose shingles. Rachel had been mortified, even at Isaac's comment that it needed a little work. That was an understatement, and a nice thing for him to say. She just couldn't figure out this *mann*.

When Miriam knocked on the door, they were greeted with the sound of enthusiastic barking. Did

Rachel notice a dog yesterday? She frowned and tried to remember but just then, Isaac opened his door. His expression did not exactly scream, "Hello, neighbors." At least he wasn't chasing them off right that second. Right by his heel was the smallest border collie Rachel had ever seen. The little animal was a lot more welcoming than his owner, wagging his tail. He barked at them so enthusiastically that his front paws flew off the hardwood floor. He was so cute, that Rachel could not help smiling, despite Isaac's expression.

"*Hiya*, Mr. Petersheim." If Miriam noticed his distaste for their company, then Rachel thought she was very good at hiding it. "We just wanted to thank you for yesterday. I heard from Rachel how you came to her rescue when she twisted her ankle."

"That so?" Isaac gave them a dubious look.

Rachel forced herself to give a thin, wary smile as she nodded in agreement. No matter how low his opinion of them was, or how skillfully he could drive her to distraction, he had come to her assistance. Of course any Amish person would've come to her assistance. It's not as if he did anything out of the ordinary. At least, that's what she kept telling herself.

"Well, c'mon inside," he said gruffly, as he opened the screen door to allow them in. "Please call me Isaac." The dog promptly ran out to circle their ankles in a quick inspection before running back inside.

The inside was very clean and utilitarian. The table was clean, but lacked a cloth or centerpiece. There were no rugs on the floors. In the living room, Rachel saw the quilt that had caught her eye yesterday. It was so warm and colorful that it clashed with the rest of the room.

"Your place is lovely, Isaac," Miriam said as she took a seat.

Isaac nodded his thanks as he offered to take the cake from Rachel and waved her to a chair.

Despite his reluctance to invite them in, he was a good host. They were served hot meadow tea and the cake, before he settled into a chair of his own.

Isaac turned to Rachel. "How's your ankle?"

Rachel felt herself jolt at the abruptness of the question, and she turned a little red. Was he Mean Isaac or Nice Isaac? It was so hard to tell. "Oh, *gut*. It's fine. *Denki*. For the ice I mean."

Isaac turned his mug of tea over in his hands. "*Gut*," he said. "I'm glad your ankle is doing all right."

"What's your dog's name?" Miriam asked as she leaned down to pat the dog, which had not left their feet the whole time. Rachel was surprised to see the dog cringe away with a whine and scuttle to lean up against Isaac's ankle. He stumbled a little on one hind leg, holding it up as he scrambled to the safety of the big man's leg.

Isaac reached down and gently scratched the dog behind the ears, his rough hands looking surprisingly gentle as he handled the spooked, little animal. "Spot doesn't care too much for people. He likes them from a distance, but it takes him a while to warm up to people."

Like dog, like owner, Rachel thought.

"Spot here showed up some months back with a smashed hip," Isaac continued. "It took near a day to get him out from under the porch. And then he had to spend a night at the veterinary clinic."

Miriam stood up. "Isaac, may I use the phone in your barn, please? We still don't have the phone connected at Eden."

"*Jah*, of course," Isaac said politely. "Please feel free to come and use my phone at any time."

"*Denki*," Miriam said. "I need to call a contractor who has a bush hog."

"You're calling a contractor?" Isaac furrowed his brow. "They get pricey this far out."

"I know. But we have a lot of cleaning up to do," Miriam said, as she made her way toward the door.

Rachel was alarmed. She was left alone in the room with the *mann* who was both rescuer and most outspoken critic all at once. An awkward silence settled between them once again as Isaac seemed to fall back deep into thought.

"Um." Rachel cleared her throat, feeling her stomach clench when he trained his eyes on her. "Did *Grossmammi* and Spot get along?"

Isaac nodded as he patted the dog in his lap. "She named him. Your *grossmammi* loved dogs."

"She sounds amazing." Rachel looked down at her hands. She found herself wishing she had known her *grossmammi*. Whatever her faults, she was her grandmother, after all.

"She would wait too, you know," he said quietly, keeping his attention carefully on the little dog.

Rachel tensed in reflex, waiting for another battle to start. "Pardon?" she said, watching him seem to struggle with his thoughts.

"For you," he said. "She figured you wouldn't be allowed to come. But she thought that when you grew up, you'd want to see her once."

"I never knew," Rachel said, blinking back the mist forming in her eyes. She bit her lip and blinked until her vision cleared. She was already babbling, and she wasn't going to add blubbering into the mix. "I never would have left her alone if I knew."

"She wasn't alone." His tone was so reassuring that it caught her off guard.

Rachel had a thousand questions about her *grossmammi* – what she was like, if she liked quilting, if she read in the evenings until she fell asleep. However, before she could find the words to ask, her *mudder* returned. "The contractor was all booked up," Miriam said. When she saw Rachel's upset face, her eyes at once darted to Isaac.

"I have to apologize to you both," Isaac said as he rose to his feet, meeting Miriam's gaze. "I was trying to bury the hatchet, and ended up making it a mess." He gave an uncomfortable cough. "I realized that I haven't done right by

Grossmammi Clara, leaving her *familye* to fend for themselves. Being neighbors now, there's just no excuse for it."

Miriam and Rachel exchanged glances. Rachel was taken aback. Did Isaac intend to help them at Eden? She wasn't sure how she felt about that.

"Anyway, I'm ahead in my work," Isaac continued. "Let me come by tomorrow with my bush hog and start on that field. I can re-shingle the worst of that roof too while I'm at it. I can help with some repairs."

"Oh, Mr. Petersheim, we can't ask you to do that."

"Isaac, please," he said to Miriam with a smile. "And that's why I'm offering. There's no need to ask."

Rachel's face flushed hot as Isaac turned his gaze on her. How could someone so cold and distant be so kind and generous too? She really didn't know what to make of Isaac Petersheim. Nevertheless, it seemed as if they were now in an unspoken truce. That at least, had lifted a giant weight off her.

Miriam smiled warmly. "*Denki*, Isaac. You have no idea how much your help means to us. You must join us for meals if you are working on the property. It'll be good practice for Rachel to cook for someone other than me before we open the house to guests. I assure you that you won't be disappointed. She's an excellent cook." Miriam fixed him with a stern look. "And I won't take no for an answer."

Isaac seemed ready to protest. Rachel could understand, seeing he was known to be distant with the whole community. This had to be a lot of human contact for him as it was. Quite wisely, however, he nodded a wary agreement. When

Miriam wanted something done a particular way, Rachel could guarantee she wouldn't let it go until it was done. Isaac had saved himself quite a battle there.

Chapter 8

It was amazing how much difference a couple weeks of Isaac's help in between his farming duties had made. The property was shaping up to look like a whole other place. The porch stairs were repaired, and so was the once weak railing. The shingles were no longer blowing in the breeze. The outside was still in need of a couple coats of paint, and the old gazebo was in a terrible state of disrepair, but the improvement was significant.

Rachel admired the newly painted guest room. She figured it would look beautiful once the newly restored furniture was brought back in. The view was looking better by the day.

Rachel leaned on the windowsill, looking over at Isaac in the field by the *haus*. Isaac was in the field plodding along on his bush-hog which was pulled by his two plow horses, slowly chewing down the saplings and waist high weeds into mulch. It would take a couple weeks, according to him. Rachel smiled when she remembered how he said that a hog has the power to deal with this sort of neglected mess, but it is as slow as tree sap in winter. Regardless, he looked to be about a quarter of the way done with the field, and that part looked so much better than the part to be done. She imagined keeping up with that field was going to be a full time job.

Isaac had surprised them both with his offer to help them out as it was, but they never dreamed he would put so much effort into his promise.

Rachel and Isaac were not exactly the best of friends overnight. He was very quiet at first, and he kept to himself most of the time. Any questions or small talk were generally met with one word responses. He tried to back out of meals the first couple days.

As the days passed though, they had gotten quite a bit friendlier. Isaac slowly started to contribute to the dinner chats with updates and suggestions. In the last few days, he had actually started talking more about himself. Rachel was fascinated to find out he had made the rocking chair she had seen on his porch, and that he was pretty well self sustaining on his property. He appeared to be a little pleased by Rachel's active interest in the fact he got by on his own for so many things.

Rachel waved as he walked back toward the house after turning his horses loose in the field. She knew that the stuff was so thick and unmanageable that he had to let the horses rest on a regular basis. Not that Isaac ever appeared to rest. He was always hard at work on his farm, or helping them at Eden. She didn't know where he got the stamina to keep up this sort of workload on a daily basis.

Rachel left the window open to air out the paint fumes, and made her way back downstairs. She glanced at the time on the grandfather clock in the living room. Almost lunchtime. She was about to start planning a meal when she realized that the lower floor smelled delicious. She hurried down to the kitchen to find her *mudder* mashing potatoes, a steaming pot beside her.

Miriam looked up when she saw Rachel. "How's the room coming along?"

"It looks great," Rachel said. "I was about to come down to make lunch."

"I've already made bread filling with pieces of chicken, and gravy, and I'm making mashed potato." Miriam dashed some butter into the potatoes and gave them a hearty stir. "You and Isaac have been working your fingers to the bone. You two take a break and go for a walk or something. I'll call when lunch is ready."

Rachel had a pang of anxiety at the idea. They were on much better terms nowadays, but she couldn't just tell Isaac to take her for a walk. "*Mamm*," she said, "I can't just ask Isaac to stop what he's doing and walk with me."

Miriam waved the wooden spoon at her. "*Jah*, of course you can. It's easy. Let me show you." She slid open the kitchen window.

"*Nee, nee, nee*," Rachel stammered in horror.

"Isaac," Miriam called. "Don't start on that dresser yet. You've been at it since breakfast. Take a break and walk with Rachel while I get lunch ready for you two."

Rachel felt her face flame red in mortification. The last thing she wanted to do was to annoy Isaac by disturbing him. "*Mamm*, I -" Rachel stopped abruptly. She knew that look her *mudder* gave her. Resistance was futile. She gave a small sigh and a reluctant smile.

Despite being shooed and practically pushed out the door, it was a lovely afternoon for a walk. The sky was clear and the weather was perfect. It had been ages since Rachel had taken a break and enjoyed a walk outside.

Rachel shot a nervous glance at Isaac. It had taken so much work to be on friendly terms, that she was afraid that he would be annoyed about being forced to walk with her. When he was angry, he was easy to read, but now, she found it difficult to know what was going on inside his head. Nevertheless, she supposed that it was better than open hostility.

"I wanted to thank you again, for all the help," Rachel said as they walked along.

To her relief, he looked faintly amused. Amused was good, especially compared to annoyed. "You've thanked me about a hundred times already."

"Um, I know." Rachel felt her face redden. She had never quite known what to say when she was around other people. Their history from the first few days didn't really help either. "But I don't want it to be forgotten. Not that you would forget. It's just I, um, I'm happy that you're helping us. That's all."

He frowned slightly and cast his eyes away to stare off at the far field. She looked down at the ground. Sometimes she wished she could be more like her *mudder*. Miriam always had a talent with words, and had a way with people. Rachel, on the other hand, could not even tell if she was irritating Isaac. "If it's all right, can I ask what changed?"

"Pardon?" Isaac stopped and looked at her.

To her relief, he did not appear to be angered by her question. He simply seemed far away, as if something had distracted him. Rachel supposed he had a lot on his mind. After all, he was putting his own work on hold to help them.

When he did not answer, Rachel pressed on. "Why did you decide to help us?" she asked, looking him in the eye to try to ascertain his reaction. "I'm not complaining, mind you. It's just, well, you have to admit, it was pretty sudden."

Rachel held her breath as she paused and waited for his response. As she expected, he appeared to withdraw into himself once again. At least it was an improvement. The last time she had pointed out how he had acted toward her, he had become cold and distant.

"I guess you could say that *Gott* laid conviction on me to see the error of my ways." His voice was somber as he looked over the field.

"I'm sorry. I don't understand," Rachel said.

Isaac fixed her with his gaze. "Your *grossmammi* Clara was a bit like you. She kept challenging me to be better than I was acting."

"I'm like *Grossmammi*?" she asked, her curiosity piqued.

"In some ways. That way you light up over stuff. The way you pushed back when I took the world out on you." He rubbed his chin as he struggled with his explanation. "But you are quieter than she was. You keep a lot to yourself, seems like. Anyone can see you have a lot of thoughts that you don't say out loud. She wasn't quite so merciful."

Rachel had to smile as Isaac chuckled at an unspoken memory.

All too soon though, that smile faded into his usual somber expression. "I'm not sure what happened between your father and Clara, but I do know that at the end, she told me she was sorry for the way she had she acted. No matter how much time passed, she always hoped to see you again. It wasn't my place to give you a hard time on her behalf. Clara wouldn't have let me get away with it. The best thing I can do know is to watch out for her girls, now that they are finally home. 'Better late than never,' she would've said."

"I wish I could have met her," Rachel said wistfully, gazing over at the house. She wondered what it would have been like to have a woman like her *grossmammi* in her life.

"I wish you could have, too."

To Rachel's surprise, he gave her a half smile. He really was a handsome *mann* and a pleasant one too, when he wasn't so guarded and distant. When Isaac was around, Rachel felt warm and safe.

Chapter 9

"So what we are looking for now is a plumber to help with the broken pipes and an electrician to fix up all the wiring," Miriam said.

The manager of the hardware store smiled. "Well, I can definitely help you out with that. So the first place you want to go is right across the street," he continued. "Old Benny has a plumbing business. He's been around for years - if anyone in town has a leaking pipe or broken faucet, Old Benny is who they call. For an electrician, make sure you go to Electrico World. They're just a few blocks down Main Street, easy to find. Make sure you tell them I sent you."

Rachel was pleased with the contacts. Both the plumber and electrician were right around the corner, so in no time they would be able to meet with them and make arrangements to get things going.

Moments later, Miriam and Rachel crossed the street and made their way into Benny's Plumbing Services. Inside were rows and rows of tools, and bolts for the toilet, showers, sinks and faucets.

Everything was neatly divided into categories, and every item was appropriately labeled.

"Hi, welcome to Benny's Plumbing Services. How may I help you today?" the friendly, young attendant asked.

"Hello, my name is Miriam Berkholder, and this is my daughter, Rachel," Miriam said. "We're turning an old house into a B&B – it's just out of town - and we're wondering if someone could come by and help us out with the pipes and faucets. A few of them are old and broken, and we really need some help repairing them before we open."

"Dad, Dad!" the young girl called out loudly, turning away from Miriam and Rachel. Her voice rang so loudly throughout the large store, that Rachel jumped. She had no idea what could have warranted this sort of reaction.

A tall, bearded man hurried around the corner. "What is it?" he asked the girl.

She rose on her tiptoes and whispered something in his ear. Rachel made out the words *bed and breakfast*. A tight knot formed in the pit of her stomach.

When their whispered conversation ended, the man turned to the two women and glared at them in much the same way the young girl had after Miriam explained who they were. The only difference was that his stare was more penetrating and intimidating. Rachel felt uncomfortable in his presence.

"Sorry, but we will not be able to offer you our services," the man said sternly. "Please leave our store."

"But we just need someone to -"

He cut Miriam off. "Sorry, we can't help you here. Please leave."

Miriam and Rachel found themselves being ushered out the store by the man whom Rachel assumed was Benny himself. She didn't know for sure as the man had not bothered to introduce himself to them.

"What was that all about?" Rachel asked Miriam.

Miriam shrugged. Her face was white and drawn. "I have no idea. Clearly there's something going on that we don't know about. Anyway, let's not worry too much about it. Come on, let's go to the Electrico World on Main Street."

A few blocks down Main Street stood Electrico World. Unlike Benny's Plumbing Service with its large and elaborate rows of supplies, Electrico World occupied a small space on the busy sidewalk, offering electrical supplies and equipment. It was a humble establishment and Rachel was certain that they wouldn't be given the same disturbing treatment as they had received at Benny's Plumbing Service.

"Hello, how may I help you?" came the voice of a middle aged man. He sported a shiny, bald head and wore a bright red polo shirt with the name *Electrico World* written in cursive on the left corner. He already seemed a great deal more pleasant than Benny.

"Hi, my name is Miriam Berkholder, and this is my daughter, Rachel. We are the ones opening the new Bed and Breakfast just out of town, and we –"

The man interrupted her and his demeanor at once changed. "Sorry, but I can't help you. Please leave!" he said, pointing to the door.

Miriam headed for the door, but Rachel stood her ground. "Why? What have we done?" Rachel asked. This was the second store they had visited for help and received the same harsh treatment. "Tell us why!" she repeated, folding her arms and standing firmly in place. She decided if they were going to leave, then she had to receive a solid reason to do so.

The man stared at them angrily, clearly frustrated that Rachel had put up such a defiant position. Finally, he let out a deep sigh. "Listen, everyone knows about your Bed and Breakfast. In case you didn't know, there is already a Bed and Breakfast on Main Street that has been around for years. That one is owned by Debra Bedshill. She's good friends with the mayor, and needless to say, she isn't too happy about your little, rustic retreat."

Now it's all starting to make sense, Rachel thought.

"Her B&B has been around for years," the man continued. "She doesn't like competition, and she's warned all the businesses and tradesmen around town not to work with you, or she'll have the mayor hike up our rent. No one wants to get on her bad side."

Rachel was stunned. She and Miriam had been had been so consumed with refurbishing the home, that it had not crossed their minds that they would have rivals in the hospitality department. They had never heard of Debra Bedshill's B&B business.

"Thank you, sir," Rachel said. She was both angry and disappointed at the revelation. Businesses compete in the same environment and for the same customers all the time. Surely Debra Bedshill didn't expect to be the only Bed and Breakfast in town forever. And furthermore, if Mrs. Bedshill was so threatened by them, bribing the local businessmen to boycott their entity was not the way to go about settling the problem.

"Come on, Rachel, let's go," Miriam said, taking Rachel by the hand and leading her out the door. "I think we've had enough for the day."

The drive home was tense and silent. Rachel and Miriam were too stunned to speak. Rachel was lost in thought.

"Just when things were looking up, this happens," Miriam finally said.

When Miriam turned the buggy into their laneway, Rachel saw a car in their driveway. They had never had *Englischer* visitors before and Rachel had no idea to whom the bright blue Ford truck belonged. Rachel and Miriam stared at each other.

Miriam drove the buggy up to the vehicle, and immediately, two figures got out of the truck beside them. There was a tall blonde woman, perhaps in her mid forties. She was wearing a tightly fitting business suit and a miserable expression on her face.

The man was tall and strapping. He was dressed in a smart, black suit and a crisp, white shirt, and looked for all the world as if he had just stepped out of an important business meeting. He seemed professional and exuded a presence that commanded attention.

The two strangers approached Miriam and Rachel in an intimidating manner which made the women immediately uncomfortable.

"Nice set up you have here," the man said in a sarcastic tone, looking the house up and down.

"I am Miriam Berkholder and this is my daughter, Rachel," Miriam said.

"Oh, my apologies," the man said, in a tone which was far from apologetic. "I am Clark Bedshill, and this is my wife, Debra Bedshill. My wife owns the Bed and Breakfast on Main Street. I am sure you have heard of it. It's been in town for years now."

Miriam nodded. "Actually, we only heard about your establishment today. We were looking -"

The woman interrupted her. "Don't you think it's quite rude to come into town and try to take over an industry that my husband and I have been in charge of for years? We were the only B&B in Town until you came along."

"I don't think there is anything wrong with providing guests with options," Miriam said calmly. "Perhaps you could have come to talk to us first, rather than threatening the local tradesmen in town not to do business with us."

Clark whipped his head around sharply at his wife. Her actions were clearly a revelation to him. She glared at him and he remained silent.

"Our place is just getting cleaned up," Miriam continued. "We are no threat to you. Why are you even worried about us? You're more established and have been around for years. We still have a long way to go. There really is no competition here."

"It is obvious that guests would choose a beautiful, countryside retreat instead of the busy main street to relax," the woman snapped. "You have the good views of the creek and the mountains behind. Guests would obviously choose your place over ours. But we aren't worried - just remember, no one in town will want to work with you on your project. They're loyal to us. Let's go, Clark."

When Rachel finished, she grabbed her husband's wrist and led him back into the truck.

"If I were you, I would pack up and head back to wherever you came from," she called over her shoulder. "No one from this town is going to help you finish this project."

The car spun its wheels, before disappearing in a cloud of dust down the lane.

Chapter 10

Rachel sat on the hard, wooden bench in the *haus* of Mr. and Mrs. Lapp, an elderly couple. The women were seated in the living room, and the men were seated in the dining room. Rachel was accustomed to this, for that happened back in Ohio when the *haus* was not enough to seat both the women and men on opposite sides of the same room. Not every *familye's haus* was big enough to accommodate the whole community every second Sunday for the church meetings. When the houses were small like the Lapps' *haus*, the ministers had to walk from one room to the other when they were bringing the word of *Gott* to the people.

Rachel and Miriam had been introduced to many people when they had arrived, but all the faces and names were lost in a blur. Rachel was looking forward to the meal after the church meeting, where she would meet the women her own age. She and Isaac had nodded to each other when they had arrived, but then she had gone to the women's room, and he had gone to the men's room.

* * *

Isaac had nodded to Rachel when he had arrived at the Lapps' *haus* for the church meeting that day. He was glad that today's meeting would not be held in a barn, or in a big *haus*, where the women and the *menner* would sit in the same room. He knew he would not be able to concentrate with Rachel in the same room.

The church meeting opened up with the singing of Hymn 76 from the *Ausbund*. As always, Amish hymns were sung very slowly, and without music. Isaac believed that this helped him to focus on each word. And, so, as Hymn 76 began, Isaac concentrated on the words.

Where shall I go? I am so ignorant; only to God can I go, because God alone will be my helper. I trust in you, God, in all my distress. You will not forsake me. You will stand with me, even in death. I have committed myself to your Word. That is why I have lost favor in all places. But by losing the world's favor, I gained yours. Therefore I say to the world: Away with you! I will follow Christ.

The words had a profound effect on Isaac. It was not the first time he had heard the words, but it was the first time that he had heard them with an open heart since Olivia had left to marry the *Englischer*.

Conviction fell upon him. *I have not trusted in Gott*, he thought, *but now I will. I will trust in Gott to perform His will on my life, however that turns out*. And, although Isaac did not want to admit it himself at that very moment, he fervently hoped that *Gott's* will for his life included Rachel.

* * *

Rachel sat in the church meeting listening to Hymn 131, *Das Loblied*. The hymn, by tradition, was always the second hymn sung in every Amish church meeting. *Das Loblied* meant "Hymn of Praise," and Rachel certainly had much to be thankful about. She was also happy that she knew that her old community back in Ohio would be singing *Das Loblied* about the same time, which made her feel connected. In fact, it made her feel connected to every Amish community, as all Amish people would be singing *Das Loblied* at that time, right throughout the country.

After about thirty minutes or so of singing slowly, the first minister started to speak. He spoke on abandoning one's will to that of *Gott*. Rachel listened to the wisdom of his words. She had thought that her life was planned for her, that she would stay in Ohio and be married to local Amish *mann*, a *mann* of her own age, not that any *menner* in her own Ohio community had caught her eye. She had no idea that she would move to Pennsylvania, or that her *mudder* would open a B&B. She had no idea that she would become attracted to an older *mann*, a *mann* who at first had been nothing if not rude to her.

Gott's ways are certainly not our ways, she thought, as she listened to the minister speaking from Isaiah chapter fifty five. *I had my life planned, but it is clear that Gott did have other plans for me.*

Two hours later, the church meeting came to an end, after another minister and then the bishop had brought the words of *Gott* to the people. Shyness at once overwhelmed Rachel, and she stayed close to her *mudder,* as introductions were made all around.

Everyone was just as friendly as the Amish folks back home. Rachel had not expected any different, but she had spent her life rarely meeting any new Amish people, so it was all a little overpowering for her. Rachel was pleased to see some girls her own age, and she was all too aware of several young *menner* her own age staring at her. She, however, only had eyes for Isaac, and her stomach twisted into uncomfortable knots when she saw the admiring glances that several of the young women sent his way.

Rachel soon became more relaxed, and chatted to the girls her own age until it was time for the church meal. As in all Amish church meals, the people ate in shifts in order of age, the oldest *menner* and women first and in separate rooms, and then the younger *menner* and the women again in separate rooms.

Rachel entered the living room, and sat down one of the wooden benches, the same wooden benches that had been used in the meeting. Some of the benches had been converted to the tables, as was the custom.

Rachel had a sweet tooth, and so, after the silent prayer, at once reached for Church Spread, a delicious combination of marshmallows, peanut butter, and pancake syrup. She spread it on a slice of fresh bread.

The other girls were doing their best to make her welcome, although she found their questions a little tiring: Did she have a boyfriend in Ohio? How did she like Pennsylvania? Had she ever visited there before? Did she have *bruders* or *schweschders*? How did she like the look of the young *menner* there today?

The last question made Rachel blush furiously, but thankfully no one noticed, or at least, had the good graces not to comment on the fact. Rachel ducked her head to hide her burning cheeks.

Anna, the young woman sitting next to her, laughed. "Mary likes Elijah, and we all like the look of Isaac, but he's too old and bitter for us."

The other girls gasped. "*Nee*, you mustn't say that, Lydia," Mary said. She was clearly embarrassed, whether about the comment that she liked Elijah, or whether about the comment that Isaac was old and bitter, Rachel had no idea, but she guessed it was a little of both.

Is Isaac too old for me? Rachel thought. *He looks about thirty. That isn't too old for me. And as for being bitter, he has certainly changed in that regard*.

As the girls chattered around her, Rachel drifted off into daydreams, daydreams about marrying Isaac, living in his *haus*, helping him with the farm, and raising lots of *bopplis*. One thing she was happy for, was that none of the girls were too interested in Isaac. She did not want competition for his heart.

* * *

It did not escape Isaac's notice that all the young *menner* were staring at Rachel. It caused a pang of heartache, a pain he had not felt since Olivia had left. Surely Rachel would prefer a young *mann*, not a thirty year old *mann* like himself, a *mann* whose *fraa* had run away with and subsequently married an *Englischer*? The young *menner* were certainly interested in Rachel, of that there could be no doubt. Isaac realized at that moment that he could not bear to lose Rachel too. He decided then and there that he would ask her on a buggy ride at the right time. *Please help me, Gott,* was his silent prayer. *Please give me wisdom as to how to go about this.*

Chapter 11

Rachel rubbed her eyes and turned over in her bed. She lay still for a few moments in a half-awake state, listening to the sounds downstairs. She wondered dreamily what her *mudder* could be doing that would cause so much noise.

At once, a louder bang caused Rachel to wake up fully. She pulled herself to the edge of her bed, jumped to her feet, and stretched out her arms. She ran down the steps and walked into one of the larger rooms, to find Miriam pacing back and forth in front of a large hole in the wall. "What happened?" she asked her *mudder*.

Miriam stopped half way through righting a chair which was knocked over, and shook her head. "*Nee*, I think we had some vandals in the night."

"I think you mean treasure hunters, or at least that's what they call them around here," Rachel said, hurrying to help her *mudder* pick up the chairs which were lying on their sides.

"Whoever they are, I hope they don't come back ever again. There's no treasure here. It's already going to take us quite a while to restore this place and open it. If it continues, it could really become a problem." Miriam shook her head once more. "I don't mean to be negative in any way, but it gets to a point where something needs to be done to stop it from continuing."

Rachel rubbed her tired eyes. "*Jah*, it does need to stop. I'm not sure when or how, but we will stop it somehow." She looked at her *mudder* and could see the pain and frustration hiding behind them. Miriam had always been a strong, kind person, but she could only hold back her emotions so much. "We should call the sheriff," Rachel added.

Miriam shook her head. "There's no phone in the house yet, of course, and the one in the barn is still in need of repair, so unless we go to a neighbor's home and ask for assistance, we'll need to go into town ourselves."

"Don't worry about that. I'll take the buggy to Isaac's *haus* and call the sheriff myself."

Miriam nodded. "*Jah*, that's a *gut* idea, *denki*. While you're gone, I'll check for other signs of damage or anything amiss."

As Rachel stepped inside the barn, she saw her bay mare. "Good morning," she said. The horse neighed, clearly expecting to be fed. "I don't feed you every time I see you," Rachel said, wagging her finger at her horse. "You've already had your breakfast."

When Rachel reached Isaac's *haus*, she tied her horse to the rail, and proceeded to the front door of the main house. Her knock echoed through the silence as the beauty of the surrounding scenery overtook her senses. When the door finally opened, she was lost in a distant stare. The sound of someone clearing their voice broke her concentration.

"Oh," she said, surprised, turning to see Isaac standing at the door. "I'm sorry. You weren't answering, so I was just looking at your property. It's so beautiful."

Isaac smiled warmly. "You're too kind." He looked out at the fields and trees. "I guess the beauty of *Gott's* creation is astounding when you stop to appreciate it. I've always seen the beauty in nature, but there's nothing like an early morning on the farm."

Rachel didn't respond, remembering why she had come.

"Oh," he said, "is everything okay? Did you need something?"

"*Jah*, actually. We woke up this morning and found that someone had been inside the *haus*. *Mamm's* taking inventory of the new damage and any other issues, but we don't have a working phone in our barn yet, so I was hoping you'd be so kind as to let us call the sheriff from your barn phone."

"Of course," Isaac said, with a wide grin. "I'm sorry such things are happening. Come on, I'll take you to the phone."

"*Denki*," Rachel said. Her mind wandered as she followed Isaac to the barn. He was so tall, and so very attractive, and now that his bitterness appeared to have left him, he was kind and gentle.

As they entered the barn, he pulled open one of the smaller doors. "Rachel, would you like me to accompany you back to Eden? Just until the sheriff can show up and take reports and all that."

Rachel tried to hide her pleasure at his words. "*Denki*. That's awfully kind of you, Isaac, but you don't have to."

Isaac smiled at her. "How could I not help such a lovely neighbor?"

Rachel's cheeks flushed at his words, and she turned away. "*Denki*, Isaac," she said shyly, still avoiding his gaze.

Isaac led her through the large barn until they came across an old, dusty phone. "Here it is," he said, stating the obvious, before wiping away a film of dirt. He then picked up the telephone receiver. He waited on hold for several minutes before being connected to the sheriff. "Good morning, sheriff. It's Isaac Petersheim, and I'm calling about my neighbors, Miriam and Rachel Berkholder. It looks like Eden, their home, was vandalized overnight." He stopped speaking for a few moments, but listened intently. Rachel tried to overhear the sheriff's replies, but they were too muffled to understand. "I'm not sure the extent of the damage, but I'm about to head back to the home with the young lady that lives there now."

He hung up the dusty phone and turned to Rachel. "The sheriff is going to come out and investigate it himself, but it'll be a bit before he can get there. He requested that we head back and wait for him."

"That sounds *gut*," she said. Rachel was pleased that Isaac had taken control of the situation as he had. Her *vadder* had died when she was young, so she was accustomed to having to do everything herself.

"Wait for me, would you," Isaac said, "so I can follow you in my buggy. Just let me harness my horse."

After the short trip to Eden, Rachel and Isaac arrived to find Miriam sitting out on the front porch. The upset look on her face became clearer the closer they got to the house. She must have found something else. The pair parked their buggies and horses and made their way to where Miriam was sitting.

"What's wrong?" Rachel asked.

Miriam's eyes met her daughter's. "I found more damage in a few other rooms on the first floor. I also noticed some things are missing."

Rachel was dismayed. "Missing? Like what? We don't even have much to begin with."

"I'm not sure of everything that's gone, but I noticed that several tools were taken, and the shovels in the barn are gone. Well, most are missing, but one was left broken in half. It looks like they were digging for some treasure all right."

Rachel felt a sadness welling up inside her as she watched her mother deal with the emotional pain.

Isaac must have felt it was a good time to break his silence. "I know it's a hassle right now, but the people that did this probably weren't aware anyone was in the home. It's because of the local lore about pirates and treasure. It's all a bunch of nonsense if you ask me, but what can you do?"

Miriam and Rachel simply shrugged.

"Miriam, if you'd be so kind as to show me the damages and where the items were taken from, maybe I can speak to the bishop and see if the community can't come together to help you both fix up these issues and replace a few of the missing items that were taken."

Rachel was pleased to see that Isaac's words had cheered her *mudder*.

Miriam turned to him with a wide smile. "There's just the one really large hole in the main room, and then there are a few spots of damages in one of the rooms by the back of the house." She motioned for Isaac and Rachel to follow her lead, and they both did so without hesitation.

Miriam took them into a large, room. She made her way over to one of the far walls and pointed to the large hole that Rachel had seen her examining earlier that morning. Isaac stepped close to the hole and touched the edges with his finger. "It looks as if they were using sledgehammers or something. Did either of you hear anything at all last night?"

Mother and daughter exchanged worried glances. Rachel shook her head as Miriam spoke. "I slept right through the night. I never heard so much as a pin drop. We were both thoroughly exhausted, though."

"Hmm," Isaac mumbled to himself as he looked into the hole.

"Well, if they were looking for treasure, chances are they walked away empty handed."

"Not entirely. They took whatever tools they borrowed with them when they fled." Miriam's voice shook. "I understand it's a part of the local lore and culture, but now that someone actually resides here, these hunters need to accept that and find a new treasure to search for."

Rachel could tell the stress was becoming too much for her *mudder*. She frowned and watched Isaac as he continued to investigate the damage.

"All right, can you show me the rest?" he said, after an interval.

"Sure," Miriam said. "The other things aren't as bad, but it looks like they broke a window getting in as well. Follow me." She walked out of the room.

Isaac and Rachel followed until they all stopped in the barn. Miriam pointed toward a window in the side of the barn. Several pieces of shattered glass lay beneath the window sill. "And that is where the tools were, all but the shovels. Who knows what else they took?" Miriam pointed toward an old toolbox that sat in one corner.

Rachel walked over to it, as Isaac's attention was captured by the broken window and the subsequent scrapes and dents that lined the wall. She noticed several empty slots in a few of the tool trays, and she was sure that those drawers had all been full just a few days prior. "I definitely think they took a few things," she said. "*Mamm*, can I look at the list of things you made for the sheriff when he shows up?" Just as the sentence left her lips, she heard a car drive up.

"Sounds like he's already here," Isaac said.

Chapter 12

Miriam, Rachel, and Isaac hurried from the barn to where the local sheriff was standing at the front door. He was an older man, with a brown uniform and a sparkling, star-shaped badge on his lapel. "Good morning," he said.

"Come on in." Miriam opened the door for him to enter. "I'm Miriam Berkholder, and this is my daughter, Rachel. I'm sure you already know our neighbor, Isaac Petersheim."

All four nodded politely to one another.

"I'm sorry it took so long to get over here, ma'am, but it's been a bit of a busy day back at the office. I'm Sheriff Dobbs. I was told there was a report property damage and a possible theft that occurred sometime last night. Is that accurate?"

Miriam nodded. "If you'd kindly follow me, I'll show you to the vandalism."

The sheriff walked behind the women as they entered the large room. He looked down at the spilled can of paint. "Was that there, or did they do that too?"

"They did that, Sheriff," Miriam replied. "They took two unopened cans as well, along with brand new tools. They also left some dents in the wall in another room, and smashed the window."

"That's probably how they escaped," Isaac added as he stood from inspecting one of the larger holes. Rachel looked over at him and nodded.

Sheriff Dobbs paced around the room silently, taking in the crime scene. He rubbed his fingers against random places in the walls, floor, and even near the windows. It was like he was looking for certain things, and then taking mental notes when they were found. Finally, he focused on the spilled paint can and crouched beside it. "It looks like this part of the vandalism at least, was an accident. Looks more like they tipped it over trying to make a break for it."

Rachel shook her head. "*Nee*, I fastened the top on myself after I used it. I even hammered it back on. I'm sure it wouldn't have opened just by falling over."

"The cover could still pop off if it was kicked or hit just right before tumbling over. If the suspects were purposely trying to vandalize the place with paint, why wouldn't they have just thrown it all over the room and walls?"

Miriam sighed aloud and fidgeted with her fingers, clearly upset by his method of thinking. "What about the two cans of paint that were missing?"

"Exactly," Rachel said. "If the people that did this were just looking for some lost pirate treasure, why would they steal paint? The tools I can understand, but paint?" Rachel tried to hide her frustration.

The sheriff scratched at his stubble. "Hmm, well I'll give you that. I've heard of those treasure hunters and looters for ages, but never do they actually take things other than what they'd assume is the actual treasure. If you were missing some gold or coins or something, it'd make more sense." He was silent for a moment. "I think it's safe to say this was robbery. Plus I don't see any conclusive evidence that would point to it being the treasure hunters."

Rachel, Miriam, and Isaac all exchanged glances. "If it wasn't someone looking for Eden's treasure, who could it have been?" Rachel said. "Have there been other robberies happening around town?"

Sheriff Dobbs shook his head. "I haven't been called to a single robbery all month, up until now that is."

"I know who it could be," Miriam said, "the B&B in the center of town. Its owners showed up here the other day threatening us and telling us we should leave and not bother opening the business here."

The sheriff's expression turned solemn. "Ma'am, I understand you're frustrated and this is a major inconvenience, but that's all conjecture. You're just assuming those things based on your instincts. In police procedure, we need to base things on the actual evidence."

"I understand that, Sheriff," Miriam said, "but the B&B has prevented us employing tradesmen. I do believe they may have tried to sabotage us. Perhaps they stole tools and paint that will not only help another bed and breakfast, but hinder us until we replace them.

And I don't believe for a moment that the paint was knocked over. It looks deliberate." Miriam pointed at the hardwood floors that were now desecrated with paint. "They didn't just tip it over. They poured it on a beautifully redone wooden floor. It had to be purposefully done." She frowned.

"Ma'am, I completely understand your points," the sheriff said. "And trust me, they make a lot of sense. The problem is that the rival owners of that other B&B are influential around here. They're even good friends with the mayor. I'm not saying that means they are above breaking the law, but even if they did, it could prove difficult to try to hit them with any criminal charges. Even something as petty as vandalism could be tough."

Miriam let out another sigh, but this one was even louder than the first. "It just doesn't make any sense, sheriff. Their establishment is directly in the middle of town, and we're all the way out here. I can't imagine we'd be direct competitors all that often."

Rachel noted that Isaac stood quiet, not saying a word, but looking on and listening intently. Every so often she would notice him looking at her, but whenever she'd catch him, he'd look away quickly. Her heart leaped when she thought that Isaac might be interested in her, but now was not the time to focus on such things. "Sheriff Dobbs?"

"Yes?" he said, turning his head toward her.

"What if it *is* the rival B&B that is behind this?"

He shook his head. "I'm going to take a report as a robbery and vandalism, but there is nothing that hints toward any one suspect." He took his hat from his head and looked around again. "How about the broken window and the other room? May I see that area?"

"Of course," Miriam said, leading him and the others to the small room at the back of the house. When they walked in, Dobbs went to the window. He stood beside it, looking out into the yard, as if looking for a path of escape or something of the sort.

"Well, this definitely could be the point of entry. Looks like it was punched or kicked in." His eyes fell upon the small dents in the wall around the window. "Hmm, not sure what that could be from."

Miriam took a deep breath. "We didn't even know there was another B&B in the vicinity until the tradesmen refused to work for us, and then they showed up here with veiled threats and harsh tones," she said. "It's clear that us being here is already bothering them, even though it will be a while before we can open for business."

"Ma'am, I'm truly sorry that I can't give you a better solution, but I honestly think it's best to just focus on repairing this place and getting it open. Once customers, visitors, and staff are mulling around, nobody, including treasure hunters and the mayor's friends, will cause you any trouble."

His words were reassuring, but Rachel could tell from the look on her *mudder's* face that she didn't feel reassured in any way.

"Is there nothing else you can do, Sheriff?" Isaac finally spoke. "I don't know too much about crime scenes and all, but isn't there some sort of method for finding perpetrators?"

Sheriff Dobbs straightened his vest. "Oh, you mean like fingerprinting? Yeah, we could do that, but I've been looking around.

There's nothing that jumps out and says, 'Hey look at me, I'm a fingerprint,' and if I go poking around this investigation by dusting all the walls and having deputies on the site, it'll become public record real fast. I think it's best if we just chalk it up as a group of treasure hunters, and if there is another incident, I won't hesitate to let the town know that we're investigating it. I'll have a forensic team here in minutes to dust for prints."

Rachel figured that the sheriff was clearly torn and unsure of what to do. "That's fine, but what about in the meantime?" she asked him.

"How do we protect ourselves from this happening again?"

"Perhaps some signs on the front lawn and doors?" the sheriff suggested.

"We've tried that," Miriam said, "but that will only help against looters."

"Well, if it'll give you two peace of mind at least until this place is up and running, I can assign a detail to come out here at intervals. Not sure how often it'd be, but you'd have a cop driving by at least a few times per night. That should be enough to scare off any would-be looters or vandals."

Miriam frowned. "I'm not sure how I feel about that."

Isaac walked over to her. "It will give you some peace of mind," he sad gently.

"I can assure you that the details won't bother you or anyone other than possible perpetrators," the sheriff said. "They'll just drive by like they're patrolling the entire town and its outer limits, and nobody but us will be the wiser. Please do keep an eye out, and if there are any more issues or concerns at all, please just call my office and I'll get back to Eden to investigate."

Sheriff Dobbs placed his hat back atop his head and readied himself to leave. Miriam and Rachel followed him out, and Isaac trailed behind. "Thank you for coming, Sheriff," Miriam said.

"I'm sorry I couldn't have been of more help. If it happens again, that's when it'll become an issue. I just don't want to you feel like you can't count on me next time."

"So, that didn't go exactly as planned, did it?" Isaac said when the sheriff had left.

"It was pretty much expected," Rachel remarked. "It's obvious that they never took steps to stop or prohibit the looters and treasure hunters, so what makes you think they'd care about some spilled paint and stolen tools?"

"I think that's the point, Rachel." Isaac looked at her. "Perhaps he needs to be sure it wasn't just a looter before he goes making a big deal out of it."

"Maybe, but what are we going if it happens again? My *mudder* is already having a hard time with all of this stress." She nodded at Miriam who was already on her knees, scrubbing at the paint on the hard, wooden floor. "We need to get this place back in order so she can be happy again."

"I'll help you with the paint," Isaac said.

Miriam looked up. "*Denki*, Isaac, but what about your farm duties?"

"I'm more than happy to help." He shot Rachel a tender look.

A thousand butterflies flew around Rachel's stomach as their eyes met.

"*Denki*, Isaac," Miriam said again. "That is so *gut* of you. I will accept your offer on one condition, that you join us for dinner tonight."

Chapter 13

As dinnertime neared, Rachel heard a soft knock on the door. It was Isaac, right on time. He stood in the doorway with a large smile. Rachel noticed that his suspenders were immaculate, which for some reason seemed funny to her, perhaps as he always seemed to have his hands dirty from some sort of work. She welcomed him in.

They walked into the dining room to a large table which was set beautifully. Several dishes sat atop the table, and a pitcher of garden tea was surrounded by glasses of ice in the center. Rachel watched Isaac as he surveyed the setting. She figured it may have been a long time before he had dinner with others.

"We're just about finished, Isaac. If you would take a seat, Rachel and I will have everything served shortly," Miriam said.

Isaac pulled out a chair. "*Denki*."

Rachel smiled and poured him some tea before helping her *mudder* finish setting the table. Once the food was all brought out, and the dinner was ready, the women took their seats at the table. Rachel smiled when she realized she was seated directly across from Isaac.

"I hope you like John Cope's Corn," Miriam said.

Isaac nodded. "*Jah, denki*. We had it often when I was a child, and it always reminds me of my youth."

Miriam chuckled. "That's never a bad thing," she said.

Isaac laughed at that.

Rachel stared at him, the way his eyes crinkled up at the corners, and the way the worry lines on his forehead all but disappeared. She closed her eyes and said her silent grace. Even though life wasn't always perfect, it was good, and it always seemed to get better, even if it was a slow process. She was so grateful that she could not put it all into words, not even in her own mind.

When her eyes opened again, she saw that Miriam and Isaac had also finished saying their silent graces. Miriam nodded and they all began eating. As Rachel took her share of the entrée, the smell tickled her nostrils. The warm smell of dried corn baked into a casserole with milk and sugar invaded her sense of smell. She thought it was a very pleasant fragrance, and the taste was delicious. Rachel had eaten like this with company more times than she could remember, but for the first time since they had arrived at Eden, she felt as if things were finally settling into place. Sure, things were still bumpy, but the road seemed clearer now than ever.

"Do you think anything will come of the sheriff's visit?" Rachel asked.

Isaac considered for a moment before replying, but he seemed hesitant even then. "Well, I've known Sheriff Dobbs for years, and he's a *gut mann*, but if his hands are tied, he won't be able to really do much."

Rachel frowned. "But it's his job to stop things like that from happening, isn't it?"

"*Jah*, but he could be thrown out of office or worse if the mayor thinks he's out to get some close friends of his," Isaac said. "Those people at the other B&B are like the type of people who will do whatever it takes to get ahead in the world."

"I understand if he can't go making false accusations, but if we come up with some actual proof that it was done deliberately, do you think he'll help us?" Miriam asked.

Isaac's eyes wandered around the room. "Honestly, I think he will do his part when and if the time comes. He's not one of the bad guys, but he's one of the good guys that are afraid to stand up to them."

Miriam sighed. "Oh well, we can have no cares for tomorrow. Only *Gott* knows what the day will bring. Let's enjoy our meal tonight."

The conversation soon turned to their old lives in Ohio. "I was reluctant to make the move in some ways, but of course I wanted to do whatever *Mamm* thought best," Rachel said.

"Oh, do you miss anyone back in your old community?" Isaac asked, looking directly at Rachel when he spoke.

Rachel thought that Isaac looked a little uneasy, as if he had just been given bad news. She was not sure if the question was directed to her or to Miriam as well. Either way, she was caught off guard by the inquiry, and had to try to hide her look of surprise. "My friends in Ohio, you mean? Yes, I certainly do. I mean, I'm sure I'll make just as many friends out here, but we lived there for a long time, so it'll always be sad in a way, you know?"

Isaac looked pleased with her answer. She could feel a warmth from him that she had not felt much of before from anyone else. Something about him caused her stomach to flutter, her heart to beat faster, and caused her to feel happy, an actual feeling of joy and happiness. While life was full of those moments, no one person previously had ever instilled those feelings so effortlessly in her.

"I know how hard it can be just to up and change your life like that," Isaac said. "It's not about how far you're dragged down, but how fast you are able to climb back up from it that matters, and speaks volumes as to your personal character. I miss a lot of things that I used to have as well, but we grow stronger and become better people because of it." His tone was gentle, yet serious and honest.

Rachel thought about Ohio and her friends. There were several whom she missed quite a bit, and even though they were far apart, those friends never left her mind.

"That is very true, Isaac. I completely agree. It's just a shame that sometimes we need to lose one or two people with whom we were *gut* friends."

He looked up sharply. "Oh, you miss someone specifically?"

"Yes. I mean, I miss them all, but I was very close to one of my friends."

Isaac seemed to be forcing a smile. "That's lovely. I hope I will have the pleasure of meeting him one day. Will he be visiting Eden when you're open?"

Rachel smiled when she realized that he was assuming her friend was male, and she had trouble suppressing a giggle. "No, you misunderstand me," she said. "The person I miss is my friend, Marie, so it's a *her*, not a *him* you'll have to meet." Rachel could not help smiling.

Miriam pulled the cover off the main dish, Chicken Pot Pie. The golden, flat crust oozed with gravy as she cut it into squares. "You mentioned that you miss what you've lost quite a bit," she said, looking at Isaac as he hoisted a large slice of the Pot Pie to his plate. "Your previous marriage?"

A solemn look lingered about his face. He looked down at his chunk of pie and then spoke softly. Rachel could tell it was an emotional topic for him. "Yes, Miriam. It's still difficult to talk about, but it caused some profound changes in my life."

"Would you ever consider marrying again?" Miriam asked, embarrassing Rachel entirely.

Isaac smiled again, but his head was down and he stared at his fork. "I had always thought I would never marry again, not after my *fraa* ran away. It's been a tough journey, but where I seem to be arriving at in life, is a place I'm happy to be at. If it's *Gott's* will that I marry another, I will not be saddened by that."

A pang of sympathy hit Rachel as she listened, but at the same time, she was a little amused by his obvious embarrassment. Isaac was such a strong, kind man. She could see through his eyes how painful the experience had been.

"Well, I think whoever that woman ends up being, she will be extremely lucky to have such a caring young man," Miriam admitted.

Rachel smiled in agreement, but tried to hide it with her hand.

Isaac's face had darkened. "My *fraa's* name was Olivia. For the first few years, we ran the farm together and had some productive seasons." Isaac paused and scratched at his eye with one finger.

Rachel was embarrassed at hearing Isaac's story, but there was nothing she could do but sit there and hear it unfold.

"We were married for some years," he continued. "Olivia

worked for a store owner, an *Englischer* by the name of Mark Lambert. She had never been on *rumspringa,* as her parents were opposed to *rumspringa* for some reason. Clearly, the pull of the *Englischer* world was too strong for her, and she ran away with Mark Lambert and later married him."

Rachel jaw dropped. "She didn't!"

"I'm so sorry that happened to you, Isaac," Miriam said. Rachel shot a look at her *mudder* and saw that she was just as shocked.

Isaac nodded, but still did not look at either of the women. "I suppose she just didn't want to live this way any longer." He shrugged. "I shut out everyone for a long time after that. My farm became just as abandoned as Eden was for some time. I lost trust in everyone, even the world around me for some time." He finally looked at Rachel, and added, "However, now I'm finally starting to feel like my young self once again."

Chapter 14

Rachel woke before dawn, as usual. She and her *mudder* sat in the kitchen each drinking a mug of strong *kaffi*. Rachel stood up to pour herself a second cup, when she heard a scraping sound coming from an adjacent room. Miriam must have heard it too, because she immediately shot her daughter a worried look.

Unsure what to do, Rachel listened closely as the noise got louder. It sounded like a scraping of some sort. "*Mamm*, do you hear that?"

Miriam nodded. "It sounds like some sort of animal."

"It sounds bigger than a rat," Rachel said, fighting her growing anxiety. "We'd better go see."

The two women clutched arms and walked toward the noise. It appeared to be coming from a closet. As they approached the closet door, the noise stopped.

Miriam reached for the closet handle. "Stand aside, Rachel, as the animal will likely run out once I open the door."

Rachel did as she was told, but when Miriam pulled the door open, all she could see was a silhouette huddled in the corner.

"Who are you?" she said.

A young man who looked about eighteen or nineteen years of age stumbled out of the closet, and then stood up. He looked stiff and sore. Rachel figured he'd been stuck in the closet for hours. Rachel then noticed a can of paint with a screwdriver sticking out of its lid right by the closet door. Clearly, he had been trying to pry the can open. "Are you a treasure hunter? What were you doing with that paint?"

she asked, while not actually expecting an answer, at least not an honest one.

"I'm sorry," he said, looking alarmed and panic-stricken. "I'm not a treasure hunter."

"What do we do now?" Rachel asked Miriam.

"I'm not sure. I think we're going to have to call the police."

At the mention of the police, the teenager's eyes grew wide. "Wait, please don't call the cops. My parents will kill me!" He sighed and took a deep breath.

"Then tell us what you're doing in our home," Miriam said.

"Um, I…" His voice trailed away. The boy looked down at the floor and let out a long breath. "I went into the closet looking for paint and stuff, but the door jammed and I couldn't get out."

Miriam shook her head. "*Nee*, I mean, tell us what you're doing here, in our home."

After a brief silence, he glanced up and spoke softly. "There's this strange guy named Aaron that works that the B&B in the center of town. He's a friend of my older brother's, so I've known him for a while. Not too long ago, he approached me and said he'd heard I was looking for my first job. He promised me a nice, paying position there if I helped him out with a little problem." The boy twiddled his thumbs.

Rachel and Miriam exchanged worried glances. "What was this little problem he needed your help with?" Rachel asked as she returned her attention to the frightened teen.

He sighed long and hard. Then, he spoke in a solemn whisper. "All he said was that management didn't want to deal with competition. He told me that he didn't want anyone to get hurt, but he wanted repairs to take a while and for any damage to be contributed to the weirdoes that hunt for lost treasure over at Eden. I think Aaron figured if you guys assumed that the looting and vandalism were the work of treasure hunters, you'd just get sick of it and leave town."

"Is this the truth?" Miriam asked, and the young man nodded. "We're no threat to them, financially or otherwise," she said. "We can all be friends and deal with each other as neighbors. There is no need for hostility or animosity."

The boy nodded. "I'm sorry, ma'am. I shouldn't have agreed to it, but I needed money, and I was just trying to get a nice, paying job with the company. I'm a good worker. I just won't get given a shot. Nobody wants to hire a kid like me," he confessed, clearly upset.

Rachel felt a pang of sympathy for the boy. "Well, if you didn't keep setting us back by destroying the property, perhaps we could have offered you a position of some sort. You didn't actually think you wouldn't get caught, did you? I doubt the stores are any more likely to hire a criminal than a struggling teenager."

The boy frowned, a solemn expression on his face. "I'm so sorry, ma'am, but please, I thought you weren't going to call the sheriff if I admitted to the whole thing and came clean?"

Miriam responded before her daughter was able to. "Okay, we will speak to the sheriff and inform him that we don't wish you to be penalized for your actions. If we see you back here, though, we're going to have to have you arrested.

We don't want to have you arrested, but we not do appreciate theft and vandalism. We work hard for what we have."

He nodded. "I'm truly sorry. You'll never see me back here again, I promise."

Miriam nodded. "We would appreciate it if you'd be willing to call the sheriff and give him your story personally."

At first, the teen looked apprehensive, but he soon agreed.

"We don't have a telephone yet, but -"

Before she could finish her sentence, he pulled a phone from his pocket. "No worries, I have my cell."

As they stood together, the young man called the sheriff's office. He spoke for at least five minutes. While Rachel could only hear his side of the conversation, the young man did tell the sheriff everything he had told them.

He hung up and turned back to the women. "So, he said he's going to check into a few things and be here later today, but that it's fine for me to go in the meantime. He has my name and contact information, so that should be enough. Again, I'm really sorry, and hope I haven't caused too much pain and damage for you guys."

Rachel sensed the remorse in his words. "Thank you for at least revealing who sent you. I think my *mudder* suspected them, but we had no proof of any sort. I just hope the sheriff thinks this is sufficient evidence for him to do something about it."

"I hope he does," the boy said, with a nervous smile. "Well, I'm going to go. I hid my bike in some bushes up by the side of the road."

"Be careful, and think about your decisions a little more next time," Miriam said.

* * *

Just before lunch time, Rachel was scrubbing away at the remaining bits of paint on the floor, when she heard a knock at the door. When she swung it open, Sheriff Dobbs greeted her with a smile.

"Good afternoon," he said.

"Good afternoon, Sheriff. Please come inside." Rachel motioned for him to enter. They walked into the lobby area to meet with Miriam.

"Hello again, Mrs. Berkholder," he said. "I got a report earlier from a teenage boy that the other B&B pretty much hired him to cause damage to the building in order to delay your attempts to open soon."

Both women nodded.

"Well, I stopped by and spoke with the manager, and he said the boy was nothing but a disgruntled ex-employee."

"What? An ex-employee? That doesn't make sense." Rachel shook her head.

"Didn't he say he was only doing it to get his first job?" Miriam asked her.

Rachel nodded, and then looked at Sheriff Dobbs. "It's true, and he didn't look like he was lying when he said it. I was looking him straight in the eyes. He was too afraid of getting in trouble to lie to us."

The sheriff chuckled. "I've heard all that before, so don't pay any attention to it. Some kids can act their way right onto the big screen nowadays," he said. "I spoke to the general manager himself. He's been the general manager at the B&B for years and he's worked with the boy personally. He knew his name, phone number, and a lot more than just that, too."

"The boy told us that the man was a friend of his older brother. That's why he knows all of his information," Rachel said.

The sheriff shrugged. "Okay, but even if that's true, there's no proof of it. I have to look at everything at face value, and there's nothing conclusive to suggest that whether the boy or the manager are being honest or lying. It's one man's word against another's. For all I know, they really did sack the kid. Then, maybe he heard about them coming here and threatening you, so he figured he'd cause some damage and make it look like they came through with their promises." Sheriff Dobbs shrugged again.

Rachel made her disagreement known. "I honestly don't feel the boy was lying to me. And besides, couldn't his statement at least help in some way?"

"Not really," Dobbs replied.

"Even if the boy is willing to be a witness, that's still not enough to at least get them to back off?" Miriam asked.

The sheriff turned his head slightly. "Look, if we find some evidence or can somehow connect them in a way that supports his version of the story, I can stop them from bothering you guys ever again, but until then, I'd suggest you both just focus on restoring this place and opening."

"Thank you, Sheriff. We're working on it, but these setbacks don't help us any," Miriam said as she walked him to the door.

When he reached the door, the sheriff turned back to face both women. "I promise, if you stumble upon any sufficient evidence, we will stop them, but right now, the charges would never stick. Not with their connections to the mayor."

Chapter 15

Another quiet morning had begun in Eden. It was a beautiful day, and the sun shone through the many windows of the building. Rachel walked back and forth, dragging a large broom with her. She swept each of the rooms thoroughly. Despite the fact that all the rooms were not yet finished, and the place was half in tatters, she still felt the need to maintain some form of cleanliness, even in the dirtiest and dingiest of places.

Rachel heard a pattering of footsteps, and looked up as Miriam stepped into the room. "Beautiful morning, isn't it? I only hope the serenity of the weather carries over into our affairs."

Despite Miriam's words, Rachel could see that her *mudder* was feeling sad. "*Mamm*, you know we must always keep the faith," she said, in an attempt to encourage her.

"I maintain my faith, and I always will, but sometimes inevitability is a real, actual thing. What if we aren't able to fix this place? We've been working very hard at it and it's still a mess. It's as if we haven't even lifted a finger. Who knows how long it might be before we're ready to open?"

Rachel rubbed her temples and thought it over. Her mother's fears were understandable, but one thing they had held onto was the idea of never losing hope. Even in the darkest of days, Rachel knew that a light could still find a person and lead them to safety. That simple way of thinking ignited her response.

"It might take us a while to get it open, but I know we will. Isaac is more than willing to help, and the community will too. You heard the bishop. They are all behind us, hoping we succeed. We can't let them down, can we?"

Miriam smiled, but her eyes were red, and she looked as if tears were in a battle to escape down her cheeks. "I think it's time we take another look at the inventory of everything we want to work on and have done to this place. We probably need to rearrange our priorities now, so the important things get completed first."

Rachel nodded. As they tossed around some ideas, there was a knock on the door. "I'll get it," Rachel said.

"Are we expecting someone?" Miriam asked as Rachel was half way across the room.

"*Nee*," she called over her shoulder.

When Rachel pulled open the door, she saw Isaac and another Amish *mann* standing beside him. The other man was older, about her *mudder's* age, and was clean shaven.

"*Gude mariye*, Rachel," Isaac said. "I hope we aren't a burden this fine morning, but my friend,

Jonas, here owns a construction company. He's from an Amish community about a hundred miles west of here."

The man extended his hand and bowed his head slightly. "It's a pleasure to meet you, Rachel."

Just then, Miriam arrived. "*Gude mariye*, gentlemen." She smiled at Isaac and glanced over at his friend. "*Hiya*, I'm Miriam Berkholder. I see you've already met my *dochder*, Rachel."

"Indeed, I have. Thank you, ma'am."

Rachel was slightly confused as to why Miriam and Jonas were smiling at each awkwardly, but paid no further attention to it as her *mudder* welcomed the two *menner* inside.

"Would you please join us for some *kaffi* and some *schnitz und knepp*?"

"*Denki*, that would be lovely, Miriam," Isaac replied.

After they were seated and Miriam had returned with steaming mugs of *kaffi* and plates of *schnitz und knepp*, Isaac spoke up. "Jonas here is a *gut* friend of mine, and he owns his own construction company. We spoke the other day and I mentioned Eden and the problems the two of you were having, and he agreed to come take a look at your *haus*."

"Oh, that is wonderful, but I'm not sure we can afford to hire contractors," Miriam admitted.

"Well, you know I'll still continue helping around here and help you both to get things in order, but you need someone like Jonas who knows his craft. Besides, Jonas and two of his crew already have a place to stay when they come to town to work – they stay in the *grossmammi haus* at the Fisher *familye's* farm."

"It wouldn't hurt to show him around and see what he thinks, would it?" Rachel said, only too aware of her *mudder's* reluctance. "I'm sure he knows a lot more about repairing these walls and doors than either of us do."

Miriam nodded. "I suppose it won't hurt to have a look." She smiled shyly. She motioned for Jonas and Isaac to follow. The first room she showed them was the one that had been the primary target of the vandalism and damage.

"Okay, so the first thing we want to do is make sure the structural integrity of the building is up to procedural standards. This hole right here," Jonas said, pointing to the wall, "could indicate that the walls might need structural work."

"Structural work?" Miriam parroted.

Jonas nodded. "*Jah*. This hole is nothing to fix, but if they have actually tried digging through to find a treasure chest, or whatever it was that Isaac said they were looking for, then these various dents and holes in the wall could have led to a week infrastructure.

That was apparent to me when I saw a few of the doorways on the way to this room."

Rachel let out a long, deflated sigh. It already looked like the bill was piling up to more than they could afford, and she knew Miriam would not be happy about it. She looked up to see Isaac staring at her.

"Don't worry too much, Rachel. Just let him look around and see what needs to be done." He looked at her with kind eyes, but the warmth behind them was not enough to erase her fears and concerns.

After taking the *menner* through each of the rooms, the basement, and a quick tour of the surrounding land, the four headed back to the *haus* to regroup. As they walked, Miriam tripped over the uneven path and stumbled backward. Jonas came out of nowhere to catch her. She fell softly into his arms.

"Oh, I'm so sorry," she apologized.

"No worries at all, ma'am," Jonas said with a wide grin. He helped her back to her feet.

Is my mudder attracted to Jonas? Rachel wondered. *He's unmarried,*

*given that he has not grown a
baard. She sure has been acting
strangely since he arrived.*

Soon, they were all sitting
together in the living room, going
over the damages, the problems,
and the additions that they needed
to have built. Jonas scribbled some
numbers on paper and after a
lengthy discussion with them all, he
finalized his estimate and slipped
the paper on the table in front of
Miriam and Rachel.

Miriam and her Rachel
exchanged glances. "There's no
way we can afford this," Miriam
said.

"With supply costs and labor, it's going to be a difficult renovation. That's probably the lowest price any construction worker could offer. I kept basic costs to a minimum, but if you both want this place to be as beautiful as it once was, it's going to be worth every cent."

Miriam nodded. "I appreciate that, and I know you would've kept the costs low, but it's just that we don't have the money. There is no way we can pay for this right now. I appreciate the gesture, I truly do, but unless we can lease out the farmland that goes with the *haus*, I don't see us being able to afford that bill. I will ask the bishop to ask the members of the community. Perhaps someone will be able to lease it. Then we will be able to have you do the renovation work. I should've looked into it sooner, but I've had so much on my mind."

"Oh yes, I've been meaning to ask you about the farmland," Isaac said. "Do you wish to lease it out just for the coming season, or long term?"

"Long term for sure," Miriam said. "I certainly don't want to do any farming."

Rachel nodded. "*Jah*, if we can lease out the land, we could easily restore this place and be on our way to opening it."

Jonas smiled. "Well, the work is going to take quite a bit of time, but you're right. This place will be worthy of being called Eden again."

The thought of that made everyone happy, even Isaac, who was clearly feeling very comfortable with Rachel and Miriam these days. Rachel considered that it was almost as if he was becoming part of their *familye*, and she could not deny how much happier she was when he was around. The way he smiled at her always seemed to cause her stomach to stir in a way which was uncomfortable yet pleasant at the same time.

"I've actually been looking for land to lease for crops," Isaac said. "Your land would be ideal, as it adjoins my farm."

Miriam turned to Rachel, her face empty and full of uncertainty. "You want to lease our land for your crops, Isaac?" she said softly.

He turned to her with a big smile. "Yes, I'd appreciate the opportunity very much. I'll dedicate all of your plots of land to my corn crops."

Rachel was unsure whether Isaac he was offering to lease their land out of his own farming needs, or whether it was his way of helping them without being too conspicuous. Either way, the notion filled her with joy, and the realization that the B&B might actually open after all, made her happy for Miriam. Eden did not look like much right then, but it meant a lot to her *mudder*, and that's all that mattered.

After a few moments of silence, Miriam finally spoke. "I couldn't imagine leasing the land to anyone better," she admitted.

Rachel recognized the look of delight in her eyes.

Isaac looked over at his friend, Jonas, and shared a smile. "Well, let's go over the details later. I'm delighted that I'll be able to lease your land, Miriam."

"I'm glad to have had the pleasure of meeting you both," Jonas said, before walking toward the exit. Isaac followed him out, but before leaving, turned to Rachel to say goodbye.

"You know you didn't have to do that," she said.

The door began to close, and right before he was out of sight, Isaac winked at her. "Yes, I did."

Chapter 16

Jonas was already hard at work with two of his crew, James, a young Amish *mann*, and Amos, a young *Englischer*. Isaac was working with them, and Rachel and Miriam were decorating the upstairs bedrooms.

Rachel and Miriam had bought new linens, towels, curtains, and carpets for the rooms, and Rachel was excited to see the space coming together at long last. The journey to this point had been filled with a few roadblocks, but she was thrilled that they were finally making progress.

It was when the two women later stepped outside that Rachel was moved to tears. It had been a long and tedious week. Jonas and his men had worked feverishly, but had not been there long. Nevertheless, the difference was already apparent.

A new, white picket fence lined the garden, while beautiful sunflowers and lilies filled the bottom. The old, brick path that led from the back porch to the garden had been excavated to reveal its original glory. It ended at a white wooden gazebo, which two weeks earlier had been a derelict building, but now was renovated in such a way that it was new, but at the same time retained its original and historical charm.

"Oh Isaac, I am speechless!" Miriam exclaimed, and Rachel looked up to see Isaac walking down the pathway toward them.

"Isaac, I can't believe Jonas did all this so fast," Miriam continued. "This is all thanks to you leasing our land. How can I ever repay you?"

"There is one way," Isaac said with a twinkle in his eye. "If your *dochder* would join me on a buggy ride tomorrow evening, I think we can settle it."

"Absolutely," Rachel whispered softly.

The following evening, Rachel looked across at Isaac as his buggy took her down a beautiful, winding lane. What she saw was a *mann* who wanted to be loved, but hadn't known how to go about finding it again. Despite his initial abrasive attitude, she had never been able to deny her attraction to him. But most importantly, she wanted him to know that his heart was safe in her hands and she would never hurt him like his ex wife had.

* * *

For a time, the two remained silent as Isaac's eyes focused intently on the road ahead. If he glanced at Rachel beside him, he thought he would become entranced with her beauty and lose sight of the road. He was still surprised at the fact that she was seated beside him.

It had been years since a woman sat in his passenger seat. After his wife had run away to marry an

Englischer, Isaac had thought that it *Gott's* will for him was to remain single. He had never imagined in his wildest dreams that he would ever fall for anyone again. Rachel was the first person in years ever to catch his eye. She was the first person to break down his headstrong, hard shell. She was the first person who had made him breathless, and he wasn't sure how to maneuver himself around her. He felt like a little boy, shy and unprepared.

* * *

Rachel marveled at the beauty of the evening. There wasn't a cloud in the sky. The lush farm lands looked greener, and the rolling hills looked more majestic. The air was fresh and butterflies danced along the grass. Rachel rubbed her arms as the cool air brushed against her skin.

Finally, they reached a level bank near the creek, and Isaac helped her down from the buggy.

"It's lovely here," Rachel said, breaking the silence.

"My father used to bring me here when I was a boy," Isaac said, "every Saturday, until he died."

"Are you anything like your father?"

Isaac smiled, a wry expression on his face. "*Nee*, my father was a gentle and loving *mann*, kind of how I used to be."

"Why are you so different now, Isaac?"

Rachel turned away from the view and faced the *mann* before her. Isaac did seem different now. He seemed shy and timid. It was a side of him she assumed that most people never got to see.

"I guess, I was hurt and I changed."

"*Jah*, but you don't have to stay angry at the world."

"True, but it was safer that way. I didn't want to get hurt again."

Rachel stepped closer to him, but she was too shy to look him in the eye. His presence was so strong and captivating that she was afraid she would never let go if he came close. "Maybe if you open your heart, you might find that falling in love again isn't such a bad thing," she said shyly.

"It's too late for that," Isaac said.

Rachel looked up at him in surprise. "Whatever do you mean?"

"I've already fallen in love," he said.

Rachel gasped.

By this time, they were mere inches away from each other. They stood face to face, as Rachel's bonnet strings blew in the wind and their eyes dug deeply into each other's souls.

"Rachel, I want to marry you," Isaac said, as his face flushed beet red. "I know we haven't known each long, but I hope we can get to know each other better, and you will then consent to be my *fraa*."

Rachel gasped and her hand flew to her mouth.

* * *

Isaac was unable to hold back any longer. The loving way Rachel stared at him and the wind blowing wisps of hair from her bonnet left him speechless. He pulled her close to him and pressed his lips into hers, causing her to melt in his arms. He wrapped both arms around her and gathered her to him, savoring the sweet taste of her lips upon his.

It was an unforgettable moment. The sun had just set against the horizon and tiny butterflies played around the grass where they stood. Isaac was overwhelmed that Rachel wanted to share her heart with him.

Next Book in this Series.

Amish Haven (Amish Bed and Breakfast, Book 2)

Now that Rachel is married to Isaac, Miriam employs the young Amish woman, Martha, to work at Eden. The vandalism escalates, the suspects again being the rival B&B owners. Yet is it vandalism, or looters searching for Captain Kidd's lost treasure?

Martha is drawn to the Amish man, James, but is James betrothed to an *Englischer*? While Martha searches for love at Eden, she first has to figure out who she can trust.

Other Books by Ruth Hartzler.

Ruth Hartzler is also the author of the *#1 Best-selling* and multiple *Kindle All-Star Award Winning* Amish Romance series, **The Amish Millers Get Married,** a series of happy, feel-good Amish romances.

The first book in the series is **The Way Home.**

The four Miller sisters are injured when their buggy is hit by a car driven by Noah Hostetler who is on *rumspringa*.

The oldest sister, Hannah, is the first to recover physically, but is left with a fear of buggies and worse still, unforgiveness in her heart for Noah.

Can Hannah recapture the love she once felt for Noah?

Will love be enough to heal the wounds of the past?

#1 Best-selling and Kindle All-Star Awarded series, *The Amish Buggy Horse*, by Ruth Hartzler.

Faith (Book 1)

For years, Nettie looked after her aged mother Elma, a demanding woman who did not want any involvement with the community.

Now that her mother has died, Nettie is alone. She is regarded with suspicion by the local townspeople, and has had no visitors from her community for some years.

Nettie's buggy horse has gone lame and has had to be retired, but Nettie cannot afford a new horse. Just as Nettie is despairing about not having any means of transport, a lost horse appears in her driveway, bringing with him far-reaching consequences.

Daniel Glick is drawn to the lonely figure of Nettie, but Nettie wants to be left alone.

However, when Jebediah Sprinkler tries to force Nettie to hand over her house, Daniel springs to the rescue.

As Nettie's struggles mount, she has to decide whether to take the law into her own hands.

And what will Daniel do when he discovers the secret that Nettie is hiding from him?

#1 Best-selling series, *Amish Safe House*, by Ruth Hartzler.

Amish Romantic Suspense

Off the Grid (Amish Safe House Book 1)

Kate Briggs is a U.S. Marshal who works in WITSEC, the federal witness protection program. After an attempt on her life, her boss sends her to live in a small Amish community until the mole in the agency is found. Will Kate, who is used to the ways of the world, be convincing as a sweet Amish woman?

When a murder is committed in the community, how will Kate assist the handsome police officer heading up the case without revealing her true identity?

And will Kate be able to leave behind her *Englisch* ways as she finds herself off the grid in more ways than one?

All Ruth's paperbacks are also available in Large Print.

About Ruth Hartzler.

Ruth Hartzler's father was from generations of what people refer to as "Closed Open" or "Gospel Hall" Brethren. Ruth's mother, a Southern Baptist, had years of struggle adapting to the cultural differences, and always cut her hair, which was a continual concern to Ruth's father's family. Ruth was raised strictly Brethren and from birth attended three meetings every Sunday at the Gospel Hall, the Wednesday night meeting, and the yearly "Conference," until she left the Brethren at the age of twenty one. Ruth still has close friends in the Brethren, as well as the Amish, both groups descending from Anabaptists. Ruth's family had electricity, but not television, radio, or magazines, and they had plain cars. Make up, bright or fashionable clothes, and hair cutting were not permitted for women. Women had to wear hats in meetings (what others would call church meetings) but not elsewhere. The word "church" was never used and there were no bishops or ministers. All baptized men were able to speak (preach, or give out a hymn) spontaneously at meetings. Musical instruments were forbidden, with the exception of the traditional pump organ which was allowed only if played in the home for hymn music. Even so, singing of hymns in accompaniment was forbidden.

Ruth Hartzler is a widow with one adult child and two grandchildren. She lives alone with her Yorkshire Terrier and two cats. She is a retired middle school teacher and enjoys quilting, reading, and writing.